MW00807877

MANSEX

MANSEX
and other stories

Max Exander

Illustrations by Richard White

Gay Sunshine Press
San Francisco

First Edition 1985
Copyright © 1985 Max Exander
Cover Design by Timothy Lewis
Cover & Interior Illustrations Copyright © 1985 by Richard White

All rights reserved. Except for brief passages quoted in a newspaper, magazine, radio or television review, no part of this book may be reproduced in any form or by any means, electronic or mechanical, including photocopying and recording, or by any information storage and retrieval system, without permission in writing from the publisher.

ACKNOWLEDGEMENTS

"Mansex" appeared originally in slightly different form in *Mandate* (September 1982). "Something to Prove" appeared originally in *Numbers* (June 1984). "Straight to S & M" originally appeared as a two-part series in *Numbers* (August & September 1982). "The Captive Connection" appeared in *Numbers* (March 1983). "Diary of a Sadist" appeared originally in *Numbers* (April 1983). "We Meat Again" appeared originally in *Mandate* (June 1984). "Club Maverick" appeared originally in *Numbers* (November 1982). "Pulses & Pressures" originally appeared in *Honcho* (March 1983). "Sir Kruger" appeared originally in *Numbers* (February 1983). "Dear Master, Dear Slave" appeared originally in *Honcho* (November 1982). "The Sex Pit" appeared originally in *Honcho* (May 1983). "Cowpoked" appeared originally in *Honcho* (October 1984). "Breakin' In At The Rodeo" originally appeared as a two-part text in *Bronc* (November 1982). "Painpleasure" appeared originally in *Honcho* (April 1983).

ISBN 0-917342-05-4 paperback

Gay Sunshine Press
P.O. Box 40397
San Francisco, CA 94140
Complete catalog of books available for $1 postpaid.

CONTENTS

for Cap

MANSEX

T HERE IS SEX, and then there is mansex. It is nothing new. Some people just say: This is the way men have sex. But is there a way that men have sex? Must they have sex at all? But when they do, there are things they feel—duplication, love, bonding, sharing, profound communication, unspoken knowledge.

In college a French woman once told me: There are many ways to make love, and each has its own special moments, its special meanings . . .

It is exquisite to feel the man beneath the shirt, to see the smile curl his lips when fingers pinch nipples, to hear the light sigh when hands probe flesh, grasp the boulder within the pants, the swelling tool which grinds against rising tool.

Tongues move from lips to ears, to necks, to shoulders. Fingers unfasten belt buckles, unbutton shirts, loosen zippers or buttons. Slowly, inexorably, the outer layers hiding the naked man peel away to reveal two men who face each other, lock eyes in deep communion, and press their lips together and say: Love.

They call us narcissists, and I won't argue. For there is nothing wrong in double pleasure, in mirrored beauty. Two male forms resemble one another and create a profound double image—though the real beauty lies in the differences.

But there are two cocks probing the air, two beautiful asses waiting to yield, to give, two individuals agreeing to come

9

together on equal loving footing, grasping, touching, wrestling—rythmically, fast, demandingly, athletically, and softly, yieldingly, romantically as well.

A rough hand moves its fingers to the soft pink flesh of a nipple, taking the sensitive tit and pressing firmly into it, pinching it, pulling it, sending waves of pleasure and spiritual disquiet coursing through the partner. Reciprocation, trading off, meeting as equals and giving and taking—this is the essence of mansex.

The pleasure of a mouth on a cock, a cock in a mouth, alternating, duplicating, ramming, sucking and licking—these are pleasures of mansex. Hands wrap around stiff meat, cradle heavy balls gently, pull, stroke, caress, yank, jerk. Deeper and faster the dicks press themselves to the back of throats, prying them open, depositing shiny pre-cum, slamming into the face with relish and vigor so that heavy balls slap up beneath the chin.

And men make decisions between themselves, decisions about fucking—to do it, yes or no, to whom? First? Second? Trade off? when the answer is yes, the mood changes, prepares, relaxes, for man will give to man, in two different, beautiful ways. Nothing is prescribed, everything is given, asked for, received. Grease and fingers and slippery cocks find holes which tense and relax, open and give of themselves for pleasure.

It goes on, it rises, it grows by the moment, higher, longer, softer, stronger. Sweat flows, blood pressure pounds, two cocks swell and beat and ooze their juices, and then a gate is opened, a frontier is crossed, and there is a certain moment when the inevitable becomes a certainty, when it is a matter of personal style only before the volcano forces its final eruption, when both men must work closely and hard, their souls meeting in whispers.

But in that one flashing moment the episode begins its ascent and descent, and the question goes unanswered in the amnesiac blast of force, the golden glory of orgasm. And then, the denouement is rapid, concluding in soft fraternity, in the embrace of strong arms, the gentle kiss of strong lips, the reassurance of loving words.

SOMETHING TO PROVE

I KNEW I HAD SOMETHING TO PROVE the moment I saw Mark walk out of the bar and climb into his truck. "So, he's back in town," I whispered to myself, watching his black Chevy roar away, peeling rubber. Still hasn't learned how to drive, I thought.

I stood there in the twilight, staring down Folsom Street and remembering. It had been two years now; no, almost two-and-a-half. It had been the coldest night of my life when he shook his head and said: "If you don't understand, then get out!" His voice barely contained the anger, and I didn't understand what he was talking about.

Well, two-and-a-half years later, I knew. And I meant to let him know that I knew. Sure, I had been a babe in the woods, but that was no justification for his brutal rejection. He could have explained, or maybe tried to educate me about the ways of mansex, but instead he threw me out.

Since then I've almost come to forgive him. After all, when a kid wears his new chaps and vest, and parades his ass around the bar with an armband on his right bicep, he had better understand just what it is that he's communicating to the other men. For that irresponsibility, for that teasing, I would forgive him for his attitude that night. But for my naivete, for my innocence, I will make no apology.

And so I stood there, the summer fog beginning to cascade

around me. Fog in this part of town means it's heavy, I thought, zipping up my leather jacket and heading for the bar. I needed a drink, and I needed it now.

I smiled and nodded at several friends when I entered the bar. Sunday evening, the last gasp of the weekend. The strange energy of the desperadoes filled the room. The Sunday leather scene has always intrigued me: an odd crowd of pleasure seekers looking for that last thrill before the cruelty of Monday morning.

I got a beer and went to a corner. I lit a cigarette and stood quietly, trying to sort my feelings. Seeing Mark so suddenly had been a bit of a shock—more so than I had first realized. The fact that I had stopped short and stood staring, instead of calling out and talking to him, must mean something. I had to find out just what it did mean.

But Sunday evening is not the time, I thought grimly, noting my friend Jack sauntering gingerly in my direction.

"Hey, babe, what's got you out tonight? Not enough action at the clubs last night?" Jack thought this was clever, sexy.

I was in no mood. "Just a beer, that's all," I said, looking away for a moment to make a face. I looked at him standing there, a little too drunk, I thought. His stance in the leather pants was a bit practiced, almost coquettish.

"That's the way!" he exclaimed, though I had no idea what he was talking about. But then I could sense that something nasty was about to slip from his thin lips. "Just came back from Seattle and first thing he's in here, looking for you!" Jack laughed and shook his head in the manner that suggests manly amusement.

"What are you talking about?" I asked. He had not said what I expected to hear. And I knew exactly whom he was talking about.

"Come on," Jack said. "Mark just left here not more than two minutes ago. He asked everybody where he could find you."

"Oh, yeah?" I said, puffing on my cigarette a bit too furiously. "You say Mark's in town?" I asked. What nonsense, I told myself. What kind of game am I playing?

"None other than!" Jack leaned close, as though to reveal

some mystery to me. "He really was hung up on you. I'd for-gotten all about it til he came in here this afternoon."

"So what did you tell him?" I asked. I had to know if Mark had gotten my new address and phone number.

"I didn't tell him nothing—other than your new address and phone number, that's all."

"Thanks, Jack, thanks," I said.

"Hell, you're in a mood!" he said and walked away, much to my relief.

Fuck, I thought, he's probably calling me right now, and here I am, trying to figure out what to do. It isn't a crisis, of that I can be sure, but it certainly seems as though something explosive is in the air.

And then I couldn't get out of that bar fast enough. I set my unfinished beer down, crushed out my cigarette, and literally flew out of the bar. I had to get home. I had to figure out what it was that I meant to say to Mark all these years.

There's no finding a bus on Sunday night, so I started to walk—fast! In a few minutes I was breathing hard, telling myself that since I hadn't gone to the gym that day, the fast pace would exercise me. Or did I intend to exorcise something? Undoubtedly, I told myself, I wanted to get rid of the growing tension brought on by the reality of an imminent confrontation. I was going to have it out with Mark.

And sure enough, when I got home the phone was ringing. I stood beside it, my hand poised on the receiver, and let it ring. But then I saw myself standing like some character in a bad movie, so I picked it up.

"Hello?" I answered, my full voice spreading innocence and light.

"Hi, kid, it's Mark. I'm back in San Francisco."

"Really? Great!" What was I saying! "Are you here for a visit, or what?"

"No, I'm back for good. Seattle is not my kind of town, I guess. That doesn't matter, though. I'm back. What's up with you?"

"Oh, the usual," I said, shaking my head at my own nonsense. After two-and-a-half years, how could Mark possibly know what "the usual" was for me?

"Yeah, well, good," he said. There was a long silence. Finally, he said, "Let's get together for a drink real soon?"

I didn't answer right off. For a split second I was ready to scream. Real soon? How dare he! Right now! I wanted him to want me now, so I could turn him down.

"How about now?" I proposed, closing my eyes and sinking into the armchair beside the phone.

"Well, okay, kid. I got your new address from Jack this afternoon. I can be there in a few minutes.

"Oh, you saw Jack?" I said, stalling for time. "Yeah, why don't you make it about half an hour, okay? I need to do some stuff."

"Okay," Mark said. "I'll be there."

I hung up and sat thinking. That'a a helluva way to tell him off. But then I realized that I really didn't have anything to say. The past is done, and what he did made sense. Oh, shit, I thought. What am I doing? What am I thinking?

And then I took a shower, scrubbing every part of me like I had to peel off a layer of something—I don't know what. Then I douched, and it was douching that brought me face to face with my real feelings. I wanted Mark. I wanted him the way I always had. The only difference was that now I knew how to do it. I had learned; I had been trained. I am a slave, and that's all there is to it.

It was this accomplishment of being a slave that I wanted and needed to prove. Mark was not the first man I had submitted to, but he was the first I had truly desired to yield to, to give fully and without question everything that he needed to take. But I hadn't known how to do it, hadn't understood that in order to give myself to a master, I had to know how to take him, how to open myself to him and his desires in ways other than simply letting him tie me up and fuck me.

That was what I had to prove, but I didn't want Mark to think I was just a good slave. I wanted him to see that I knew my prior innocence had hurt him, and though I couldn't apologize for what I hadn't known, I could yield to him in such a way that he would understand I was not to blame for what had happened two-and-a-half years ago.

But his rejection had hurt me. My defenses rattled at the memory, but still I knew it had been the hardness of his rejection that had forced me to discover what I had needed to know.

I could think no longer, because Mark's footsteps were pounding on the wooden stairs. I opened the door, and all six feet of him was there, as handsome and muscular and sexy as always. His jeans were worn and tight, his big dick pressing a long line down his leg. His shirt was tight and sexy, his chest— that incredible chest—pushing against the fabric.

It was a long moment of lust, pure and simple. I knew why I wanted him. And I was naked. I hadn't dressed after showering and douching. I wanted to confront him in this way, honestly, without pretense or props. The look on his face was startling: he smiled, frowned, looked me up and down. It was an unusual way to greet him, I knew.

"You look good," Mark said. "The gym has worked for you." He came in and passed his hand behind my neck.

"Really, it's the other way around," I said, feeling excitement and anger at his touch.

He looked around the place for a minute and lit a cigarette, never once looking at me. Then he turned suddenly and said, "Why are you naked?"

I had not expected this question. Or rather, I had not expected it so directly. "Because . . ." I faltered. "Because I want you. It's that simple."

"Is it?" he asked, looking into my eyes and then down at my cock.

"Do you want me?" I asked.

Two honest sentences from my mouth: *I want you* and *Do you want me?* It was enough to drain all my energy.

"Yes, I've always wanted you," he said, looking down at the floor, then back at my cock. "But . . ."

"Yes, but . . . but you didn't want me enough to teach me, to explain what I didn't know, what I couldn't see . . . ." I could not go on.

"But I did teach you, the moment I told you to get out. You learned right then what you needed to know, but I knew it would take time for you to become conscious of it."

I couldn't answer; there was nothing else to say. There was only something to prove, but the timing was off. We couldn't just fall into a sex scene. But my dick was getting hard. And his dick was getting hard.

We stared at each other across the room for a long moment. I said nothing, but my face told him to do it, to start again. Mark was silent, appraising the situation—wondering, I am sure, how to begin again.

"Two years ago," he said, "we were standing just like this." He looked at my dick, which was already hard and thrust heavily into the air between us.

"Yes, and I knelt and put my hands behind my back...." I started to kneel, but he cut me short.

"Don't!" he said. Mark put his arms around me protectively and held me tight for a moment. "Please..." he whispered, and then he kissed me, his moustache brushing my lips, his mouth opening against mine, his tongue probing my mouth and finding my tongue. The kiss was deep, passionate, long. His hands ran over my shoulders and down to my hips. Then he grasped my erection.

I fumbled with Mark's clothes and soon we were both naked. His muscles rippled beneath a fine pattern of soft brown hair. His dick—that huge weapon—hung heavy, half hard, its veiny, knotty thickness curving down and brushing my thighs.

We kissed and brushed our lips along each other's necks. He bent his head down and licked my nipples, teasing them into firmness, and I reached down and stroked his huge cock, amazed at its length and thickness as it rose imperiously between us.

Mark led me to my bed, pushed me down on it, and laid himself on top of me. I opened myself to him, wrapped my legs around his back, felt his dick press between my legs. He kissed me deeply and pushed the throbbing knob of his dickhead against my asshole. There was no lube, but somehow I opened fully to him. His monstrous thing slid into me, pried my hole wide open, and buried itself to the hilt.

He fucked me hard and long, pulling his prick all the way out and then plunging it back in with a force that made his balls slap against my asscheeks. I could feel him take possession, the incredible sensation of our bodies locking together as his powerful hard-on rammed into me again and again. My ass loosened and grew slick, and Mark's tool probed deeper, harder. He bit my nipples and yanked on my balls, taking my body in a furious, fabulous, violent way. I thrust my hips forward to take him in, to let the surge of that massive penis penetrate me as deep as it could.

There was no turning back, no recoiling from the insistence of the moment. He possessed me fully, but in that same act I possessed him. He was also the instrument of *my* pleasure. His bucking increased and every thrust tore me open wider, spreading a tingling sense of sexual relaxation through my pelvis and belly.

His hand on my dick pumped tight and fast, my own precum making it slick and slippery. We both erupted in a shuddering climax. In that last instant before his cum shot wildly into my hot ass, before my cum creamed into his hand, he whispered "I love you." I echoed the words, realizing for the first time what it was that he had wanted me to know, to understand, so long ago.

He pulled out, leaving me empty, but we lay there wrapped in each other's arms, drenched with sweat and cum.

"This is how we begin," he said. "The rest is yet to follow."

I knew he spoke the truth. I knew he was now willing to possess me, to use me as his slave and lover, and I also knew that I had proven to him what I needed to prove: that I was willing to accept his love.

STRAIGHT TO S&M

JEFF AND I HAD BEEN FRIENDS for nearly four years, ever since we had shared a big house with five other guys in college. For about a year we hadn't seen each other much, because I had graduated a year earlier than he, but once he got finished with school, he moved down to the city and found a place to live just a few blocks from my place.

So we had continued our friendship, drinking together, swapping sex stories. He was straight, and I always got a kick out of hearing about his adventures with chicks; he knew my scene and really enjoyed hearing about my nights at the clubs or other special scenes my friends and I dreamed up.

Jeff worked summers as a lifeguard, his tall muscular frame perfectly conditioned by hundreds of laps in the baking summer sun. He was fair and handsome, his jaw angular and strong. He was by far one of the best-looking men I knew. I often joked that if he decided to go gay, I got first dibs on that gorgeous ass and big dick of his. He always laughed and agreed.

One day another friend and I were sitting around bored shitless, when he thought up the idea that we should make pornographic pictures of ourselves in compromising positions and send them to a mutual friend of ours as a joke. Our mutual friend was a sleazy bastard, and we knew that he'd really go for the pictures.

Once the pictures were taken we had to figure out how to get them developed—we didn't trust the commercial firms. I remembered that Jeff had a hobby of photography so I called him up to get him to develop the pictures. He said sure, so we met at a darkroom downtown and did the photos.

Afterwards, at home, we were looking at the photos all spread out around us. Jeff pointed to some of them that showed me with a cock ring on and asked about that. I said it was a real kick, he should try it sometime. And then I went and got it and threw it to him. He said he didn't know how to put it on, so I laughed and said, "Do you want me to show you how?"

"Sure," he answered.

I stopped and stood there for a minute, a wry smile crossing my lips, uncertain if I ought to just show him a thing or two.

"We always have this little stand off," he said, "to see who will back out first."

"Okay!" I said, determined to get him to chicken out as I reached for his zipper and belt. I undid the belt buckle, un-snapped the first button, and hesitated, waiting for him to back out. Then I realized that sure, fine, I'll put the damn thing on him, that's all, very clinical and matter of fact, simply a demon-stration of the procedure. I unzipped his pants and pulled them loosely around his hips. I pulled his shorts down and widened my eyes as I saw one of the biggest cocks I've ever seen, getting bigger by the moment.

"What if I get a hard-on?" he laughed.

"What if . . . " I said, as my hand cupped his balls. He smiled at me and leaned back as I wrapped my hand around his thick cock. At this point I could hardly believe what was happening with this "straight" man, but it sure as hell felt alright.

I held his thickening prick in my hand for a long moment. My mind was a jumble; after all, this was a good friend of mine; we had been friends for three or four years; he had never once shown an inkling of desire for me or for any man before, and yet here I was, his long hard tool clutched in my nervous hand. I debated in my mind what my next step should be—should I suck him, should I kiss him, should I have a "little talk" with him?

What I did instead was lean down and give a quick lick to his big balls. He moaned in pleasure, my signal that everything was okay, that he wanted me to go on. So I did, starting to work my hot tongue around his heavy hanging balls, licking under them and between his legs, and then up and around to the base of his cock. He sighed and laid back further, widening the spread of his legs. I positioned myself in front of him and started to lick up the base of his cock, along the underside of the shaft, a good eight inches from bottom to top.

Being a blond Germanic type, he had very little hair on his body, and his cock and balls were smooth and silky, except for two or three throbbing veins coursing through that monster of a dick. His rock-hard body seemed chiseled of alabaster, conditioned by years of swimming and diving in his mountain hometown.

My tongue reached the top of his dick and lapped at the drop of liquid pre-cum there. I took the head of his dick in my mouth and sucked it, got it wet, and then began to take more of the huge organ in my hot mouth. He sighed again and said, "Man, I'm so fucking horny and this feels so good."

I swallowed the whole thing with these words of encouragement, delighting in his moan of pleasure at what I later found out to be his first experience at being deep-throated, at having his whole long fat tool inside someone's throat. Later he told me that no chick he'd ever been with could suck dick like that, and I had laughed and told him the ancient dictum that if it's a blow job you want, send a man.

I continued to suck his dick, and wondered just how far this thing would go; would he fuck me? Would I fuck him? Little did I know what was in store for the rest of the evening.

He started to move his hips back and forth, thrusting his manhood in and out of my mouth and throat. I reached up and played with his nipples. He practically shot his load on that one; I guessed he had never had his tits played with and I was right. He moaned in ecstasy as I pinched and lightly pulled on them, all the while his dick slid in and out of my mouth.

"Suck it baby," he whispered, and it was at that moment that

I began to feel the anger inside me. Was I going to sit here and be a goddamn blow-job machine? Was I just going to be some little faggot friend of his that sucked him off so that in the middle of some liberal talk he could say to his girlfriend, "Oh, yeah, I let a guy suck me off once . . . ."—just to prove that he's such a stud he's tried it all?

And just as I was about to stop, to say something, I felt his hand lightly caress the back of my neck, then pass down to my shoulder. His touch was tentative, exploring, betraying his confused emotions about responding, about going ahead and expressing his desire, after all, for another man, for me. He passed his hands across my shoulders and down along my arms, feeling the tight muscles there, and then he touched my chest, the way one bodybuilder touches another, testing, touching for muscle, for strength, and then I felt the tension leave him, a moment of slight hesitation (that moment of crossing-over), and suddenly his fingers were on my nipples, gently touching and rubbing them, fingering the soft pink points that he knew so well from his own man's body, and now found with such pleasure in my body.

I lifted my mouth off his dick and leaned back, reaching forward to finger his nipples as he fingered mine. He smiled at me, a funny, crooked little smile, and I recognized us there, our hands on each other's tits, just like so many male couples everywhere throughout time.

And then his fingers pulled away from my chest, pulled out from inside my shirt, and gently, slowly, he began to unbutton my shirt, lifting it away from my shoulders and letting it drop on the floor. I realized that this man was ripe for the picking, that he was feasting on the opportunity to be so close to another male. His eyes roamed over my chest and shoulders and upper body. I knew from the look in his eyes that my hours at the gym had paid off—he, the straight man!—was feasting on my masculinity! This was a powerful aphrodisiac, and my raging hard-on pressed full force against the denim of my jeans. I could tell from the look in his eyes that he was ready to try it all, and when he looked down at the fat bulge along my thigh, I knew that he was eager to get the touch of another man's prick on his body. He ran his hands over my chest, across my hard stomach, back up across my nipples, and then, in a hesitant but swift single motion he put his hand on the bulge in my pants and felt the hardness of another man's big dick fill his rough hand.

He rubbed his hand along the length of my stiff cock, squeezing and pressing it with his strong hand, and then reaching up to unbutton my jeans. He worked the buttons open, one by one, and then pulled off my jeans. I lay naked, my huge cock throbbing against my belly, and I felt his hands pass along the inside of my legs, closer and closer, and then, in one sudden motion once again, my dick was in his hand, my balls in the other. He stroked my hard-on and kneaded my balls, his hands trembling at the new sensation of feeling a hardness to match his own. I mimicked his activities, and we sat there for a long time, straddling each other, playing with our cocks and balls and occasionally grinning.

"This is just like playing when you're a kid," he finally said, laughing. "I love it!"

"Yeah, it is just like kids," I said, taking his cock into my mouth once more. I laid out flat beside him and felt his warm breath on my crotch. I sucked his dick for a long time while he lay and watched my hard-on ooze its pre-cum. Then he said out loud, "Ah, what-the-fuck," and the next thing I felt was his hot mouth sliding around my dick, sucking it into the warm depths of his virgin mouth, and in just a few seconds he had mastered the art of sucking dick.

We worked on each other for a long time, and then he stopped. He pulled me up next to him, took my face between his hands, and roughly began to kiss me, his tongue probing between my lips and searching for my eager tongue. He held me tight, as if grasping, reaching for something, and then he relaxed, pulled away, leaned down to suck my tit. I kissed the top of his head and fingered his nipples as he first took one nipple in his mouth and then the other, sucking and biting and licking it, driving me to the edge of orgasm.

But then he stopped. He sat up and gathered his knees up

against his chest and just sat there. I didn't know what was going on, or why he had stopped, but I feared that this was it, the straight backlash against some supposed seduction. I resolved not to say anything, lest I touch off some strange sequence of emotions. We sat silent for a few minutes, although his hand was still resting against my leg, a gesture that comforted me somehow.

Finally he said, "Man, this is great and all, but it's just not . . ."

"Just not what?" I asked, expecting him to answer something about women.

"It's just that I always pictured something different from a situation like this. I mean, you know, this is nice and all, I like it okay, but it's not much different from doing it with a chick."

"Thanks!" I said, indignant.

"Hell, no, I mean you're great. I love all that muscle and that fat cock of yours . . . ."

"So?"

"So, the thing is, I sort of expected something more like these pictures here, or like that stuff I've looked at in those magazines you're always reading, you know, stuff like that. That's what I thought sex with guys was all about."

So that's what he wanted! He wasn't going to have sex with a guy if it was going to be just like sex with a girl. If he was going to have sex with his buddy, he wanted some all-out raunchy hardcore man-to-man action. I considered this for a moment, made a snap judgment and barked out an order.

"If that's the way you want it, then down on your knees motherfucking cocksucker."

He looked up at me and laughed sheepishly, but the sudden slap across his face convinced him that I was for real, that I expected my orders to be fully obeyed.

"That's what you asked for, fuckface, so you're going to get it. Now down on your knees!"

He scrambled to the floor and got on his knees, his face turned expectantly.

"Look down at the floor, slave," I ordered. "A good man-slave does not look at his Master unless ordered to do so. Got that?"

"Yes . . . ." he muttered.

I slapped his face again. "Yes Sir! is how you will answer me. Got that?"

"Yes Sir!" he barked.

I could judge by the enormous stiff prick jutting out from his body as he kneeled there that he was fully enjoying the scene. I could see that he was anxious to get into some real man-sized action, and I wasn't about to disappoint him.

"Okay, slave Jeff, you may begin by repeating after me: I am your slave, prepared to serve you as you see fit." Jeff repeated the words after me, and I could see that they had a profound psychological effect. His stiff prick started oozing pre-cum so much that it formed a silky stream from the tip of his cock to the floor.

"Get your face down on the floor and lick up that drop of pre-cum," I ordered. "Any messes you make on the floor you will have to clean up, with your tongue."

He bent down to the floor and stuck his tongue out to lap up the few precious drops of clear liquid.

"That's real good," I commended him. "Looks like you're a born natural, won't need much training."

He came upright again and I ordered him to put his hands behind his back. He did, and I grabbed a length of rope, tying his hands together at the wrists behind his back. His eyes sparkled as he looked down and watched me fixing the rope around his wrists. He moved his hands to test the bond and found that he was indeed my captive.

"Okay, slave, sit on the floor, on your butt, and spread those legs apart."

He did as I told him to, almost losing his balance as he sat, unable to stabilize himself with his restrained hands. Once he was down on the floor, he spread his legs wide apart and waited. His big balls hung so low that they were now resting on the floor, and his thick cock still pointed straight up towards his belly.

I stepped up to him and touched the toe of my black cowboy

boot to the head of his dick. The clear juice clung to the boot and I lifted my foot to his lips, ordering him to lick it off. He lapped at the boot like a child given candy, and then I brought my boot down across his cock, slowly pushing it down and away from his body, pressing it along the floor. His balls flattened out on either side of his swollen member, and as I pressed my boot harder against his dick, he writhed in ecstatic discomfort.

"You feel that cowboy boot grinding your puny dick into the floor, cocksucker?" I asked. "How'd you like this boot grinding your balls into the floor, huh?"

"Uh, Sir, I . . . ."

"What, slave? Say it."

"Please, Sir, grind my balls into the floor with your boots."

I slid my boot off his cock and watched it spring up against his belly again. I placed my toe against his balls, pushing them around the space between his legs with the tip of the boot. He said nothing, sitting rigidly watching my boot push his balls around on the floor. I stopped moving my foot then and started to press down, firmer and firmer, until I could see that the pain was causing his prick to almost shoot its load.

I finally let up and ordered him to get on his knees again and crawl to the edge of the bed. He did, and when he got there I told him to bend over the bed, with his ass sticking up in the air. He almost hesitated, but a swift slap on the ass made him bend over the bed, his round, hard virgin ass stuck right out into the middle of the room.

I knew that being a straight man he was most worried about his ass, so that was the part I most wanted to get busy. Break his ass and he'd be a great slave. Leave him a virgin and he'd stay proud, too much straight-stud attitude. But I realized I'd have to awaken in him the latent desires all men have to get it in the ass.

I ran my hand over the smooth hard globes, feeling the firm muscles, kneading and pressing them with my fingers. I lightly slapped them a couple times, something he obviously enjoyed, and then I ran a finger down the crack of his ass and over his unused hole.

He shuddered in new-found pleasure as I fingered his hole. I didn't try to insert my finger; I figured he'd be too uptight for that, and I wanted to open him up with my tongue anyway. I played with his ass that way for a long time, until he started to visibly relax his body and there was a subtle hint of movement in his hips as I continued to fondle his asshole and balls.

When he was plenty relaxed I kissed his right ass-cheek, and then I kissed the left one, gently trailing my tongue up and down the split between those perfect half-mounds. I slid my wet tongue down to his hole, then beneath it by his balls, and then slowly I placed my warm tongue on that tight little hole, gently rolling it around and around, tasting the sweat and musty staleness of his body. He moaned in unbelievable pleasure as I worked my mouth on his asshole, sticking my tongue inside his hole just a bit, and then darting it in and out, faster and deeper each time. He started to rotate his hips and roll his ass around in unison with my tonguing motions in his hole. I could feel the hole relax, open just a bit, and then open more, sliding around my tongue as he tightened and loosened his hole, testing all the new found sensations of his ass.

When he was really rolling and moaning I stopped and grabbed a can of grease, gently inserting one and then two fingers into his relaxed, waiting hole. He sighed again, then said:

"Please, Sir, may I say something?"

"Yes, Jeff," I said, making sure to be non-committal in tone.

"Please, Sir, I think I, uh . . . I think I'd like you to fuck me."

I could see that it was a big step for him, and I replied by sticking another greasy finger up his ass and saying:

"You're gonna get it, don't worry. You're gonna get fucked real good."

By now I had all four fingers up his ass and he was moving his hips up and down, just begging for more.

"Tell me to fuck you," I ordered.

"Please fuck me, Sir," he answered.

"How much do you want it?" I asked.

"I want your dick up my ass, Sir, please."

I started to rub the head of my thick cock against his greasy loose hole, gently pressing the round end right against the asshole, pushing slightly without entering him.

"You really want this dick, man?" I asked.

"Yes, Sir, I want to feel what it's like to get fucked."

"Beg."

"Please, please, Sir, fuck me. I beg you to stick your dick inside me." He gasped as I stuck the head of my dick into his hole and held it there.

"Is this what you want?" I asked just as I pulled the head of my dick out of his ass again. "You want me to stick this big monster dick up your hole, just like you used to stick that monster dick of yours inside some chick?"

"Yes, yes, yes Sir! Please fuck me!" he shouted, desperately horny by now.

"Okay," I said, "you asked for it." With that I sank my full, thick eight inches into his ass, watching as my big dick slowly disappeared into the wet hole. I eased it in, inch by inch, as he wiggled his butt to take it, amazed and pleased all at once that it didn't hurt at all, not one bit, that it felt damn good sliding up inside him, filling him up and making him hornier than he had ever felt before in his life.

I started to pump with short gentle strokes, waiting to feel his hole relax that one last bit, that extra centimeter or so that would signal it was time to plow that man-hole with all my might. I slid my dick in and out of his ass, mildly fucking him and watching his rock-hard body relax and move to adjust to all the new sensations and experience of being fucked by a man.

Then, as he moaned and whispered something like "please, Sir, I love it, or love you" or something like that, I felt the tension leave his ass, felt the silky softness open up to my invading prick, and then I began to let loose with some heavy fucking. I thrust my loins against his ass, my long thick dick shoved against his prostate. I could feel the hot slick walls of his ass clinging to my dick, and I pumped harder and harder, shoving it in and out with as much force as I had. He bucked and ground his hips. He looked desperate to jerk off, but his hands were still tied behind his back. I grabbed hold of his bound wrists, using them as leverage to really thrust my raging hard-on deeper and harder into his ass.

"Feel that big dick shoved up your ass, slave?" I yelled. "Feel what having sex with a man is all about?"

"Yes, Sir, I love it, Sir, I want nothing but dick up my ass. OOOOh please, Sir, fuck me, I love it, I love you."

I pulled my dick out of his dripping hole and let go with a hard smack across the ass. He yelped and I slapped him again. "You fucking cocksucker, you do not love your master, you serve him only!" I reached over for my belt, doubled it in my hand and started to beat his ass.

His blond ass-cheeks reddened quickly, but I could see that he was enjoying the beating; his hips continued to rotate and thrust backwards to meet the swing of the leather belt against his hard ass.

I climbed up on the bed and stationed myself in front of his face. My dick was covered with grease and ass juice, dripping thick pre-cum.

"Suck me off, slave. I'm tired of fucking you and I want to cum. Suck me off and drink my cum."

He looked up at me for a moment before opening his mouth and taking the bloated meat into his hot mouth. He sucked on my dick, bringing it to complete erection, fully thick and raging hard. I fucked his face, holding his head with my hands, shoving my greasy cock in and out of his slurping throat.

"Oh, yeah baby, suck that dick," I said, forcing his face further onto my cock. He swallowed it down, sucking and rolling his tongue around the base of my cock buried deep in his throat. "Suck it!"

Then, I knew I was about to shoot another load into his mouth. I fucked faster and harder. "I'm gonna shoot my load, slave, I'm gonna cum in your mouth. You're gonna drink my cum, man, drink it all you cocksucking sonofabitch."

I shot a huge load of boiling cum into his mouth. He swallowed and swallowed as I pumped more and more of the hot white cream into his throat. I fucked his face until every drop was spent, until he had milked my cock dry of cum and swallowed every drop.

I sat back and smiled at him. "Whoa, that was one helluva fuck," I said.

I looked at him and saw that he was really horny, but there was another emotion in his face, too. He looked angry, mean, and I climbed off the bed, untied his hands and knelt on the floor beside him. Placing my hands behind my back, I looked at the floor and all I said was:

"Your turn."

"What did you say?" Jeff asked me, looking down at me as I knelt on the floor beside him.

"Your turn, Sir," I said, looking up at the man I had just fucked and abused, at the straight man I had just turned out.

Jeff smiled for a moment, probably thinking of all the things he could do with me to get even for my rough seduction of his virgin hetero ass. I could read his face—he was thinking of the early tender moments that had quickly given way to the heavy, raunchy mansex, when I had tied him up, whipped his ass, and fucked him silly with my big cock.

There was no doubt about it, he was savoring the few moments of consideration as he debated in his mind just how he intended to have his revenge, how he intended to show me that he had discovered that yes, this was what he had always wanted.

Slowly, he stood up, stretching his arms above his head, yawning, looking me over as I knelt naked beneath him. His long prick was half-hard, hanging heavy over his big nuts, dripping plenty of shiny pre-cum from the heavy fucking he had just gotten. He dropped his hands to his side, then reached forward and stroked his long tool in front of my face.

"Like that dick in your face?" he asked.

"Yes, Sir," I answered. "Please use it on me."

"I will, man, you can be sure of that." He yanked on his dick, now standing stiff again. "Believe me, I am going to show you just how much I enjoyed having you fucking rape my ass. You're gonna know you just had yourself a straight man."

"Yes, Sir," I said, trembling slightly at the hard edge in his voice. He was damn serious.

"But I ain't straight no more," he continued. "You just took care of that once and for all. And since this is the first ass I'm gonna fuck, and the first male-mouth I'm gonna get service from, I'm gonna make it count. This is gonna be one helluva evening."

He circled round behind me, grabbed the length of rope that had bound his hands, and roughly tied my wrists together, pulling the knot tight and making sure I couldn't get free.

"Got any more rope?" he asked.

"Yes, Sir," I answered, "in the closet."

"Good," he said, walking over to the closet and rummaging around until he found the other piece of rope.

He bent down and tied my ankles together tightly. He stood back to look at his handiwork.

"Not bad," he said, "not bad at all. You're pretty fucking helpless like that, man; I can do just about anything I please . . . like grab your balls and squeeze the holy shit out of them." As he said this he swiftly reached down between my legs from behind and grabbed my heavy nuts, tugging back at them and grasping them like a vise with his rough strong hand.

He squeezed hard, yanking down on them, causing me to almost topple forward, since my hands and feet were tied together helplessly. "Ya like that, boy? Ya like getting some attention from your straight friend?"

"Yes, Sir," I managed to gasp as he gave one final tug on my nuts and then let them go. I relaxed my body for a moment, only to feel him push me forward with his foot, forcing me to the floor on my belly.

"Yeah, you look real good all trussed up and laid out like that," he said. "That hard round little ass is really pretty."

I lay waiting for his next move. I felt his foot run gently up the back of my thighs, his toes gently nudging me and digging into the cleft of my ass. He pushed his toes towards my asshole, moving his foot up and down. I began to grow hard again, and I could feel that need begin to well up within me, that special need to feel a man's hard cock in the ass.

He took his foot away and said, "I'm going to enjoy fucking that hole, I really am."

He knelt down beside me and ran his hand over my helpless body. He ran his hand across my back, over my thighs, and then over my ass. I felt his warm hand pass over first my left ass globe, then my right, then he pushed his fingers between my legs and worked his fingers around my asshole.

Suddenly, he hauled off and slapped my ass, leaving a stinging red mark.

"That's for the way you treated me, slave," he said as he raised his hand and slapped my ass-cheeck again. "You beat my ass with a belt, fuckface, and I want your ass to be just as red, just as hot." He spanked my ass with full force, whacking first one side and then the other, making my ass red and burning from the beating.

My meat grew stiff, throbbing up against my stomach as it was pressed into the floor. The beating was really turning me on, it felt so good to feel those rough slaps on my rock-hard butt. I started to move my hips up and down to meet his slaps, and the caressing of my throbbing dick against the floor really turned me on.

"Okay, roll over," he ordered, turning my body over. I lay on my back and looked up and him kneeling beside me.

"Yeah," he said, "you're all mine, baby." His eyes roamed over my body, across my broad muscular chest, down my flat belly, across my rigid meat and big globes.

He reached out with both hands and pinched my tits, pulling them, and kneading them, and twisting them between his thumb and forefingers. "Ya like that, don't you? Feels good having your friend pinch your tits?"

I nodded and closed my eyes, revelling in the wonderful sensation of the pleasurepain coursing through my body. He moved his hand to my hard cock, grabbed it with both hands and squeezed it hard. I felt him stroking my dick, and then he let go and straddled my body. I opened my eyes and saw his thick organ hanging above my face. I could feel the heat of his pulsing erection and thick ball-sac on my face, could smell the salty dampness of his groin.

"I ought to piss in your mouth right now; you guys like that stuff, don't you? I remember one of your stories I really liked was when you and that big bodybuilder got into the beer and piss scene one night. That really sounded far out."

He rotated his hips, drawing his giant sex closer to my lips. I opened my mouth, ready to submit to anything this man wanted. But instead he inched forward and lowered his ass onto my face. The hot hole was still wet from my fucking, smelling of cum and sweat.

"Eat it, man, eat my ass," he ordered. I stuck my tongue up his ass, rolling it around the outside of the soft hole, then gently inserting the tip into the relaxed sphincter. I could taste my own cum there, and he moaned in pleasure as the soft tongue probed his stimulated hole.

"That feels so good, man, so good . . . ."

I kept at it, rolling my tongue around, sucking my cum out, fucking the ass with my hot soft tongue. He writhed and moved his ass up and down; his cock bobbed up and down on my forehead, and his balls rested across my eyes and the bridge of my nose. I was in ecstasy serving this hunk of man, my old college buddy.

"Wow," he said, pulling himself off my face. "I'm so damn horny I can't wait to get into that ass." He sat down on my stomach. "But I've got to have just a little more fun first."

He ordered me to get up on my knees, and helped me into position. "Okay," he commanded, "lick my body all over, starting with my toes."

"Yes, Sir," I said, bending over to take his toes in my mouth. I covered them with hot spit, sucking and licking one foot and then the other, and then licking up around his ankles, calves, knees. I licked the inside of his thighs, licking up to the groin and back down again, covering his body with warm, wet spit. I reached his balls and began to lick them, taking the big bull-balls in my mouth and sucking on them. When I began to lick his cock, he moaned and said couldn't wait much longer to shove it up my ass.

I sucked and licked his rigid tool, feeling the long pole slide down my eager throat as he began to fuck my face. He withdrew his erect member and ordered me to finish licking his body. I worked my tongue up his strong muscled abdomen, pausing to stick my tongue into his navel, then following the thin line of blond hair up his belly to the heavily muscled chest. I licked the bottom of his huge pectorals, running my tongue along the definition of the muscle, then licking up around his armpits, then across the chest, circling slowly and carefully around the small round nipples. I licked around the edge of the pink circle, slowly working my tongue closer and closer to the erect tip of the nipple, and then all at once I was tonguing his tit, working my tongue fast over the small bullet of flesh. He moaned and pulled my head against his chest.

I finished and licked my way to his armpits, wetting the hair there and smelling the heady aroma of his healthy athletic sweat. I licked up around his neck, and then he took my head in his hands, brought his lips to mine, and kissed me roughly. His hot tongue shot into my mouth, fighting with my own tongue again, tasting my cum, his sweat, the mustiness of his own ass.

"Fuck I'm horny!" he said, picking me up and throwing me onto the bed. I landed on my back. He jumped on top of me, wrestling me like a kid, but my bound hands and feet made me just a plaything for him, a toy to be wrestled and rolled over and used.

"Alright!" he said when he rolled me over onto my stomach and ran his hand down across my hot ass. "I'm gonna fuck the shit out of you. If you think you gave me a fuck, wait til you feel this piece of horsemeat stuck up inside you!"

He reached into the can of grease and pulled out a big glob, spreading it onto his pulsing dick, then coating my hole with a healthy mess of the lube. He stuck a finger into my asshole and finger-fucked me hard, sticking a second and third finger in and working my ass wide open. Next thing I knew he was climbing on top of me, untying my ankles and spreading my legs wide. His hands spread my ass-cheeks apart, and then I felt the head of his engorged penis positioned at the waiting hole.

"Ready to get fucked, slave?" he said, resting the end of his cock against my hole.

"Yes, Sir, please fuck me," I said.

"I wanna know you mean it," he said, slapping my ass with his hand.

"Please, Sir, *fuck me*," I said, moving my ass back onto his dick, trying to eat the huge weapon with my hole.

"I don't think you mean it," he said, leaving his cock pressed at the threshold.

"I mean it, you asshole . . . I mean, Sir, I really want . . . beg you to fuck me . . . shove it inside me, Sir, I want to feel your throbbing dick pounding inside me, Sir. *Fuck me!*"

"Yeah . . . ." he said as he sank the whole fucking monster dick deep into my ass. He slid it in with one long sudden thrust, and I forced my ass back against his belly, my steaming ass consuming the thick rigid sex weapon. He began to pound my ass at once, showing no mercy as he rammed his slab of dick into my ass.

He lay on top of me, wrapping his arms around me and fingering my nipples as he pumped his hard-on into me, shoving and bucking his swollen penis as hard as he could into my butt.

"Oh, take it, slave," he said. "You fucking take it just like I took it from you. I know how good it feels to get it up the butt, and I'm just fucking giving you your fair share of the evening. Oh, yeah . . . ."

He pounded harder and faster, ramming it deeper with every thrust. My hips moved back and forth, eagerly accepting impalement on the burning sex sword, begging for more with each ram.

"Please, man, fuck me, fuck me, shove it up my ass, man, take me, yeah . . . shove it inside me . . . ."

"Oh, yeah, baby, that slave ass likes a man's big dick, don't it . . . ."

"Fuck me, mister, fuck me, give me more . . . ."

"You're getting it, fucker, take it, take this huge dick from a hunky dude . . . you worthless ass, fucking slave-hole . . . take it . . . ."

"Fuck me, shove it up my ass, c'mon, fuck it, fuck it . . . ."
He shoved his dick in and out, sliding it into my burning
asshole, slowly and then faster. Then he began to slow, to take
shorter strokes, and then, inexplicably, he stopped and pulled
his dick out.

"What's the matter, Sir?" I asked.

"Nothing," he said, "nothing at all." He reached into the
grease and grabbed another glob. "I just got a better idea, that's
all."

As he started to smear the grease over his whole hand and
wrist, I knew what he had in mind. I was ecstatic at the thought
of his shoving that big athlete's hand into my ass and pounding
it there.

He inserted four fingers at once with no problem. The heavy
fucking had opened me up real good. "Yeah, that's good," he
said as he pumped the fingers into my loose greasy hole. "I'm
gonna shove this fucking fist up your ass, just the way you like."

I took a deep breath and pressed down on his hand, begging
him to fistfuck me like a man. He closed his hand into a long,
thin arrow and maintained a steady pressure while my ass opened
up to accept the hand. I suddenly realized that my best friend
was sticking his hand in my ass, and the thought aroused me
so that my ass opened up completely. I breathed deeply and
relaxed, surrendering myself to him for his pleasure and use.

The incredible sensation of being filled up like never before
flooded my senses and I groaned in pleasure as his hand disappeared into my ass. The greasy hole closed around his wrist
and he gently began to massage my anus, pushing his hand in
and out.

This stud had taken possession of me as completely as any
man can. I lay beneath him, my hands bound closely behind my
back, my ass upturned and impaled on his invading arm. I
moved my hips first one way and then the other, in order to fully
accept this gift of manhood, this offering of indescribable
pleasure.

"I'm gonna jerk off," he whispered, and I shuddered at the

thought of feeling the hot white cum shoot onto my back as he fucked me with his fist. "I'm gonna stick my dick into your ass and jerk myself off inside your ass . . . ."

I nearly lost consciousness at the thought of this hunky dude sticking his big fat dick back into my ass inside his closed fist and fucking me like that.

"Please," I whispered, "do it; do anything you want. I give myself to you, I want you to take me, to fuck me, to jerk off inside me. I'm yours, man, yours . . . ."

Neither of us made a sound as he positioned his dick at my invaded asshole. I felt the pressure of his cockhead on the hole, then felt the opening of the hole as his dick slid in along side his wrist. Inside me I could feel the throbbing staff sliding in, forcing its way into the tightly closed fist.

Finally he leaned down and kissed my neck, whispering in my ear that he was jerking himself off inside me, that it felt damn good, that it was the best, the very fucking best sex he had ever had. I was in another state as he slowly approached orgasm, breathing heavier, becoming more and more intensified as he slid his dick in and out of his fist buried inside my burning hot ass. I felt him gasp and stiffen, then I felt an incredible heat in my ass, a molten sensation of burning liquid as his hot cum poured out of his body into mine, pumping his essence deep within me, flooding me with his masculinity.

We lay silent for several minutes, and then he gently pulled his dick out, followed by his hand. It was an odd, sad feeling as all the fullness slowly left me, but I knew that he had flooded me with himself, had cared enough to give me all that he had. Mixed with the knowledge that in the same night he had fully abandoned himself to me and absorbed my manhood, I knew that we were solid, that we belonged to each other.

THE CAPTIVE CONNECTION

"**W**HAT WAS THAT you said, asshole?"

The muscular leatherman leaned close against the bar, his mouth at Todd's ear. "What'd you say you wanted?"

"I . . . I . . . uh . . . I want to be trained," Todd stammered, reaching for his beer, uncertain about coming on to this handsome man in leather.

Another leatherman grabbed Todd's wrists and held them tight behind his back. "Listen, fucker! When your Masters ask you a question, you answer us with a respectful *Sir!* Got that?"

"Yes!" The grip on Todd's wrists tightened. "Yes, *Sir!*"

The two leathermen grinned at each other behind Todd's back. The kid had been eyeing them all night, unaware that the two hunks were fuck buddies out looking for a young slave.

"That's good," the leatherman holding Todd whispered, loosening his grip somewhat but still firmly holding him captive. Todd was frightened by their sudden move on him, but his long cock was nearly hard, nevertheless, pressing painfully against his tight jeans.

None of the other men in the dark bar seemed to notice; if they did, no one would care. Dominant mansex is what this back-room scene is all about—the captive connection, the giving and taking of pain and pleasure.

Disco music throbbed in the place, casting a numb, primitive aura across the bar. A swath of red light cut across Todd's face, and he looked up at the tall hunk grinning at the leather-

man who continued to hold Todd captive.

"We'll fucking train you good, buster! We got a place all fixed up for fuckers like you! Come on!" With that the men steered Todd through the mass of musclebodies and smoke, shoved him out the door, and dragged him into their black pickup. Todd noticed how the truck smelled of leather; the upholstery was shiny black cowhide.

They drove through the dark warehouse district. Neither said anything, though the one kept Todd's wrists held tightly. Todd was still frightened and his cock throbbed, spreading a dark blue stain where the pre-cum oozed under his jeans.

Why am I doing this? Todd wondered as they rounded a corner into a dark alley. Why do I want to be a slave? The truck pulled up in front of an old apartment building. Todd stumbled out and was dragged into the building. It was uncomfortably warm inside, and suddenly they were climbing stairs, Todd being pushed ahead with his arms still painfully wrenched behind him.

He did not panic. He loved every moment, cherished the force. He knew, or suspected, that he was about to find exactly what he had been looking for, for a long time. The leathermen unlocked a door and shoved Todd into a well-equipped playroom. In the dim light he was surrounded by reflections of himself and his Masters. The walls were mirrors. In the center of the room were a low table and sawhorse. Todd's prick oozed plenty of pre-cum when his eyes saw the rope and chains and many leather devices to be used on his body.

"Okay, kid, strip!" The studs stood back and stared at Todd, who wavered for a moment. They spit on him and slapped his face as he began unbuttoning his shirt and unfastening his jeans, revealing his sweaty, muscular, youthful body.

"Good, boy! Ya got a nice little body there." One of the leathermen walked up and circled Todd, who stood nude in the center of the sex room. "I am Master Mark and this is Master Tex." Todd said nothing, but he did manage a slight nod. He looked at Tex's crotch and noticed how large the blue jeans were beginning to swell.

Tex was all his name implied: tall, lanky but muscular, with reddish-blond hair and a handsome chiseled face that was somewhat weathered. Mark was the classic leatherman: a huge, dark stud in chaps, with a big black moustache, hairy chest and enormous muscles. Exactly the kind of men Todd liked—strong, hunky, masculine, ready to take control and use him as a plaything.

But why? The thought crossed Todd's mind again. Why do I want to be used as a plaything? As a sexual toy? Why do I want to take orders? There was something there, some memory that was trying to surface. Maybe the only way to figure it out was to get on with it and try to bring it out by reliving it. Was that it? Todd forgot his thoughts as Master Mark's rough hand flew through the air and whacked his ass.

"Ow!" Todd yelped as the sting spread through his butt. Again the big hand slapped his ass, then again on the other asscheek. "Beg for it!" Mark commanded, his raised hand waiting to strike again.

Todd fumbled and didn't answer for a second, but then he gave in to the scene and consented. "Beat me, Sir! Fucking beat me!"

"You asked for it!" Tex said and pounced on Todd, grappling him to the floor. He held Todd's torso firmly in place as Mark slammed a hand across the slave's naked ass.

"Take it, baby, take the beating!" Mark said, slapping the hell out of Todd's ass. Tex reached around and found Todd's little pink nipples, grabbing them between his rough fingers and twisting.

"Oh . . . please!" Todd moaned, but he knew to shut up. It was almost instinctive.

"Get up, asshole!" Mark commanded as Tex crossed the room to grab a rope.

"Get over to that sawhorse!" Mark ordered. "Now straddle it!"

Todd obeyed, his balls pressed flat against the wood, his hard dick sticking straight up in the air, his strong hands gripping his tense legs.

"Got some piece of meat there, huh?" Mark said, wrenching Todd's throbbing dick around like a toy. "Well, it ain't nothing compared to the equipment Tex and I have got."

Tex returned with a length of rope and several strips of leather. "Tex is an expert with rope," Mark said menacingly. "Speaking of my big dick, I want you to get it out and suck it!"

Todd unfastened the jeans and they burst open from the intense pressure between Tex's legs. His eyes widened at the sight of the huge, fat manmeat in his face.

"Like that big dick, slave?" Mark asked, forcing his fattening prick into Todd's face. Todd began to suck and slurp on the huge tool, feeling the long pole slide down his throat. Again, a memory flashed through his mind, something similar yet different, something that was driving him to pursue this experience, this sado-masochistic thrill of sexual release.

As Todd sucked, Tex tied his ankles to the back legs of the sawhorse. Todd felt the rope pull his legs backwards and he winced when the wood burned his flesh. The pressure forced him to lean forward into Mark's crotch. Next, Tex wrapped the rope around his slave's wrists and pulled Todd's arms above his head. He secured the rope to a beam in the ceiling.

Mark slammed his enormous prick in and out of Todd's mouth, causing the cocksucker to gag. Next a wide leather strap was placed across his belly, just above his stiff cock. It was pulled up and back, lifting Todd's hips away from the sawhorse. With his ankles tied behind him and his hands tied above, Todd felt the pressure of the belt completely support his hips, forcing his pelvis to tilt forward. Todd realized he could not move his hips forward, and his butt was held up in the air by the leather strap. But as he sucked, he found that he could move his hips backward, away from the strap.

Tex delivered a hard blow to Todd's captive ass, leaving a wide red splotch. Next thing Todd knew, his balls were being wrapped with a leather cord, then tied to the sawhorse. It was painful and extremely binding; the leather strap held his hips up, the leather cord pulled his balls down. He was stuck.

"Suck that big dick, boy!" Mark groaned, slamming his cock

in and out of Todd's face. Tex connected clamps with a chain to Todd's tender tits. Then he fastened the chain to the sawhorse. This pulled Todd's body forward at a difficult angle. He was almost parallel with the sawhorse now, his throat and ass completely exposed at crotch level.

Mark pulled his dick out and stood back and then walked around to survey Tex's handiwork. "Good fucking job, Tex," he said. "Damn good!"

Todd saw himself in the mirrors and his dick sprang higher at the sight. Yes, he thought, this is it. This is what I want—to be tied up and used, tied up so I can't move, so I have to do whatever they want.

"What do you want to see him doing, Tex?" Mark asked his buddy. Todd realized that so far he had not heard Tex speak.

"Well, I'd like to see him get fucked good and hard," Tex said slowly, deliberately.

"Sounds fine," Mark said. "I'm pretty fucking worked up anyway." With that brief announcement, he positioned the head of his throbbing cock against Todd's tight asshole, probing it gently and then sliding his whole piece of meat deep inside. Slowly, Mark began to pummel the ass, thrusting in and out, slapping Todd with his hands, making the tender flesh burn red hot. Tex stood by, stroking his own long tool and looking like he was fixing to join in.

"I'm ready to fuck," Tex announced simply. Mark pulled out and Tex put his hard cock against the hole. "Wanna fuck, kid?" he asked, watching Todd raise his hips to try to get the dick inside him. "Yeah, kid, I can see you do. You really do!"

Tex pushed the slippery head of his dick into the hole. He withdrew a moment, dipped his fingers into a can of lube, and slapped his cock into the hole. Then he shoved his dick all the way in.

Todd moaned as the rapier stabbed him, but Mark's fat prick suddenly stuffed his mouth and muffled the cry. Todd was completely captive, completely at the mercy of these two studs.

And then he remembered, and he was amazed that he had ever forgotten those afternoons after school, when he and the boy next door used to play "concentration camp." Bobby would lock him in the basement and tell him to get naked before he returned. But he would always come back right away, before Todd could strip, so Todd would have to finish stripping in front of Bobby and then take whatever punishment his friend deemed adequate. Usually he would squeeze Todd's dick until it hurt, or he would slap Todd's little balls hard and laugh when the boy curled up in pain. Sometimes he would punish Todd by tying him to the legs of an old stuffed chair stored in the basement. Then he would leave Todd alone, tied up and naked, without knowing when Bobby would return.

The leathermen fucked Todd's ass and mouth hard as he hung suspended, bound and helpless. He felt a fullness, a completion, as though he had come full circle and was finally at peace in the captivity he enjoyed. The moment had come for Todd to abandon the unremembered and deliver himself to his sexual destiny. *I am a slave!* he thought exultantly. *I am a slave!*

Mark rammed his dick down Todd's throat while Tex shoved his huge tool up Todd's ass. Todd moaned and sucked, feeling the pain in his tits, his balls, his ass.

"Hey," Mark said to Tex, "I'm about to shoot, but I want to do it in his ass. Let's switch."

"All right by me," Tex said, yanking his long piece of meat out of the greasy shit-chute. They changed places and before Todd could think, Mark rammed his huge dick in the hole and Tex slid his greasy pole down Todd's throat. Todd tasted the funky sweat and grease on the big dick that had been fucking his ass, and it made him suck all the harder.

The leather dudes pumped his holes, stuffing him full of hard manmeat, and Todd's dick was a fountain of pre-cum. Mark really rammed it home, moaning and holding onto Todd's hips, shouting "I'm going to come!"

"Yeah, baby, flood that ass!" Tex prompted. "I'm gonna shoot this mouth full of hot white stuff!"

They rammed their pricks into the hot softness, harder and faster, beating their meat into explosions of cum, filling Todd at both ends with white liquid, burning his tongue and rectum with hot jism.

"Fucking good slavemeat," Tex said, pulling his dick out and letting it swing in front of Todd's face. "Think we gotta get this guy off?"

"Sure," Mark said, yanking his bloated dick out of the tight asshole. "I'll jerk him off. You gonna watch or work his tits?"

"Good idea," Tex agreed, reaching under the bound man and pinching his tits roughly. Mark reached beneath Todd's belly and stroked the raging hard-on, spreading the copious pre-cum over the swollen prickhead, and Tex yanked on the tits with his hard, tough hands.

Todd was crazy with lust. He was being jerked off and his tits were being worked on good. It took only a few minutes to bring him to the boiling point. He greedily accepted the attention of these two studs and shot his hot load all over the sawhorse and the floor. His mind flashed on his boyhood buddy, and he realized that somewhere, right now, Bobby might also be a captive connection.

WOODCUT

I T WAS A SIMPLE WOODCUT PRINT. But it had been his undoing. Oh, had it ever. As Tom Markman swung the little black Alfa Romeo Spyder into his driveway, he considered what it was about the print that had got him going.

It was not so much the craft of the art itself that impressed him, though it was exceptionally good. Nor was it the content: two cowboys on the range, leaning against a fence and watching their horses. But there *was* something there in the conception of the scene, something in the artist's vision of the cowboys together. It had got to Tom.

And when Tom had met the artist—it was the opening of a showcase of Western artists—he had felt a rush of some strong emotion, something akin to love and greed and frustration and lust.

For it was this type of man—this artist—that Tom found most attractive. And as it so often seems, it was this type of man Tom found most difficult to attract.

The man's name was plain enough: Jack Dorn, a name which Tom couldn't place ancestrally. Was it English? Dutch? Swedish? Well, Tom thought as he slammed the Alfa's door and started to put up the top, it doesn't really matter. What really matters is that the man turns me on.

And so Tom stopped to consider just exactly what his feelings were about Jack Dorn. The man turned him on, that was a starting point. But that feeling of being "turned on"—what did it consist of? Jack was certainly very good looking, tall and muscular, handsome, masculine. But the package wasn't the whole picture, because there was something sparkling in Jack's eyes that had touched Tom's feelings, had stirred up affection and lust, surely a dynamic combination.

Tom looked at his watch. It was still early. If he called the gallery he might be able to reach Jack before he left for a party or something. But no, Tom thought as he opened the door to his apartment, I can't phone some guy up and ask him out, just like that. He stepped into his living room, furnished so sparsely with ultra modern pieces; but now, it looked more empty than fashionable, more stark than simple. He looked at his watch again; there was time.

He went to the phone and pulled the gallery's business card out of his pocket. He dialed the number, but just as it was about to ring, he hung up. He couldn't do it, just couldn't pick up the phone and call like that. He went into the bedroom and hung up his camel-hair jacket. He slipped the Ruffini shirt off and let it fall to the floor; then he stepped out of the light wool slacks and hung them up. He kicked the black Italian shoes into the closet and stood before the mirror, examining himself in just his Calvin Klein undershorts. He smiled in self-amusement as he compared himself to that man in the Calvin Klein posters; frankly, Tom thought he was much more attractive than the poster boy.

Tom appraised his muscled body, not too overdone, but just right. The proportions were perfect, smooth and well-defined. He slipped his jockey shorts off and stared at his naked body. Pretty nice, he whispered, looking at the perfection of his genitals. They, too, were in perfect proportion, not so overly large as to appear vulgar monstrosities, but so perfectly shaped and proportioned as to inspire gasps of awe at the beauty. His dick began to harden in his self-contemplation, fattening just a bit, stretching the satiny-smooth skin of the organ into a tantalizing half-hard shape.

It was that slight edge of horniness that got him going again. He went to the bedroom phone—a black cordless wonder—

and dialed the gallery.

"The Clark Gallery," a young woman answered. Tom could hear the gala in the background; it was less raucous than when he had left. He hoped he hadn't missed Jack.

"Yeah, hi," he said, "I was just there, and I wanted to talk to Jack Dorn for a minute, if he's still there."

"Let me see if he's gone yet," she said, and then, "Oh, I see him, he's still here; hold on."

Tom stood there naked, holding the phone, waiting for Jack Dorn to come to the phone. His hand started to shake, and his cock fattened up a bit more. He wasn't sure what he would say.

"Hello, there," Jack said. "Who is this?"

"Hi, it's Tom Markman. I just met you earlier at the show, you know, I'm kind of blond, in a camel-hair jacket . . ."

"Oh, yeah, I remember," Jack cut in. "I remember you fine."

Tom inhaled sharply; his dick thickened perceptibly. He glanced at his nude reflection as his hand trembled at the receiver held to his ear.

"Well . . ." Tom began.

"Yeah, well," Jack said. "I'm about to sneak out of this madhouse. Where are you?"

Jack swallowed. "I'm at home." He hesitated, just slightly uncertain, then: "Why don't you stop over for a drink?"

"Okay," Jack agreed. Tom was stunned. He had expected something else, perhaps to meet at a bar or a club; he hadn't expected Jack to agree so eagerly to meet him. But of course, he was thrilled. After giving directions to his place, Tom hung up and stood naked before the mirror, uncertain what to do next. Finally, he put on a pair of jeans and a black sweatshirt, then turned the lights in the bedroom down low. He went into the living room and put the corner lamp on, creating a soft, seductive glow.

Just right, Tom told himself, hoping that Jack was the sort of man his art suggested. It was the conceptualization of hardness, of a tough male world of cowboys, miners, laborers that bespoke Jack's potential as a lover for Tom. Tom wanted it good and male, hard, tough, maybe rough, too. He waited, and then, after a few minutes, a cab pulled up in front and deposited Jack. The bell rang. Tom stalled for only a moment, then opened the door. Jack stood there, smiling, a little drunk. "Invite me in," he said, stepping through the door. They smiled at each other, and Tom took Jack's coat. He re-examined the young artist's body, surprised that he hadn't noticed earlier how heavily muscled it was. Jack saw that Tom was appraising him; he knew he'd like what he saw. Jack looked at Tom, briefly, seeing that he was, as he had recalled on the phone, exceptionally attractive, with the look of one of those GQ models.

"Offer me a drink?" Jack prompted, already enjoying the cat and mouse they were playing. Tom poured him a drink and brought it to him. Jack took it, letting his fingers lightly touch Tom's as their hands passed the glass.

And then it began, almost instantaneously. Jack circled Tom, under the pretense of looking at the room. Tom knelt on the floor, under the pretense of finding a coaster that had rolled beneath the couch. Soon, Jack's crotch was positioned in front of Tom's face, and the ensuing behavior was unpredictable, wild. Jack thrust his bulging basket into Tom's face, and hornier than all hell, Tom eagerly began to munch on the bulging jeans, his mouth closing and chomping on a thick tube beneath the tough fabric. His hands roamed up across the narrow hips, then along the tight torso, circling the nipples which poked little bumps in Jack's shirt. His fingers toyed with the tits through the cotton, while his mouth munched on the big basket stuffed in his face.

Jack pushed Tom away and helped him to stand. They came together in a passionate embrace, their lips meeting, their tongues probing each other's mouths, tasting, feeling. Their hands roved, grabbed, tugged, and finally, they were both naked, their torsos wrapped together with muscular arms, their bellies meeting with each heavy breath, their thickening pricks rubbing between them. They were busy exploring their mouths, their tongues flickering and caressing their lips, the tips of their tongues.

Slowly Jack began to kiss his way down along Tom's neck, inching his hot lips closer to the sensitive nipples. Then he circled the pink point of flesh with his hot wet tongue, circling the erect nipple, then flickering lightly over it. Tom moaned his pleasure as he felt the warm lips close over his nipple. Then Jack moved further, kissing a damp trail along Tom's muscled belly, then down the firm abdomen to the erect cock, so beautiful, so perfect.

Jack gently licked around the base of the beautiful organ, letting his tongue flick dog-like on the balls beneath. Then he began to lick up along the underside of the stiff shaft, finally reaching the thick head and closing his hot sucking lips around it. Tom pushed his hips in an involuntary motion to bury his hard cock in the soft sucking mouth, and Jack hungrily slurped at the big thing. Before long, Tom was shoving his stiff pole in and out of Jack's throat, getting off on the hotness of the artist sucking his rod. But he knew that he had to stop Jack, or else Tom would shoot his load too soon. And he had plenty more in mind.

Tom pushed Jack's head off his dick and sank to his knees, even with Jack. Their lips met again, their tongues poking into each others' mouths, hands grabbing, sweat running from their foreheads, their armpits. "Fuck me," Tom whispered as his hand wrapped around Jack's stiff meat. "Fuck me in the butt good and hard; take me," he urged. His hand sensed Jack's enthusiasm as his dick leaped at the suggestion.

Jack pushed Tom back, so that he lay on the floor; he raised Tom's feet to his shoulders and wrapped his arms around Tom's legs, locking them in place in the air. With gentle probing, his finger found the tight, slightly damp asshole and began to slide in. "Oh . . ." Tom moaned as he felt his legs held up in the air and Jack's finger probing his hungry asshole.

After a few minutes of finger-fucking, Tom's ass was wide open and eager. He watched in lust as Jack stroked his thick piece and aimed it at Tom's waiting hole, and then, in one long and lusty movement, Jack lowered his hips and guided the stiff pole inside Tom's butt, eliciting cries of pleasure from them both. Tom rolled and raised his hips against the invading prick, passionately eating the long, thick pole with his hot ass, letting the monstrous sex weapon slide all the way up inside his slippery hot rectum.

"Fuck me, baby," he whispered to Jack, who began to slide his meat in and out, pummeling the tight asshole. He leaned forward and kissed Tom, then dropped his mouth to Tom's tits and began to bite and nibble them, bringing the pink flesh to full erection while he continued to pound the ass.

Jack slapped Tom's asscheeks as he rammed his cock deeper and deeper, then grabbed his balls and yanked on them, pulling Tom's loins more fully onto his fucking shaft. Tom's perfect cock lay up against his belly, its beautiful purple head throbbing and oozing pre-cum onto his belly. Every thrust of Jack's massive cock caused Tom to moan, and his dick would spring up, then slap back against his belly.

Before long, Jack was ramming the meat hard and fast, fixing to cum and blast a hot searing load of jism up into Tom's slippery butt. "Shoot it," Tom prompted, as Jack rammed harder and wrapped his fist tight around Tom's waiting cock, starting to pump it off as well. Both men reared and bucked, flailing about in lust as their big dicks prepared to shoot their hot loads. Just as Jack felt his balls churning and the cum begin to rise, Tom's cock responded to Jack's rapid jerking-off, and together, they both groaned and began to squirt big hot loads of burning white cum. Jack's hot man-liquid flooded Tom's ass and sent his own orgasm even higher, as Tom's beautiful cock swelled up thick and purple, squirting gobs of hot sperm over his chest and stomach.

Jack eased his pumping and brought his face down to Tom's chest and stomach, licking up the cum, lapping at the hot liquid as it trailed down his belly and ribs. Then, they kissed, Tom tasting his own cum in Jack's mouth.

For a long time they lay wrapped together, with Jack's cock growing softer inside Tom's ass. But then, finally they kissed and took a shower, only to return to the bed for more action.

"I'm glad you cut prints of cowboys on the range," Tom told Jack, referring to the gallery opening hours before.

"I'm glad you appreciate art," Jack answered. But the conversation was cut off. Jack's big dick was getting bigger, and Tom knew what to do about that.

DIARY OF A MASOCHIST

F OR YEARS I HAVE FANTASIZED about sadomasochism, about being the object of hard sex. When, as a teenager, I would jerk off, I'd play vivid scenes in my mind of sexual degradation, but always at the hands of a woman. I don't know why this was the case. For some reason my gay fantasies were always romantic; I wanted to be loved by a man. But I wanted to be enslaved by a woman.

Whenever I could, I'd pick up a copy of the old BERKELEY BARB, pouring over the "de Sade" column, dreaming of a time when one or two dominatrices would force me to strip, serve them, and then jerk myself off in front of them.

As my fixation on men became more cemented, and as I developed an identity as a young gay man, these heterosexual fantasies gave way to visions of brutality at the hands of men.

But I could never actualize these fantasies. They were deep and hidden, never shielded from myself, but always shielded from my friends. It seemed that none of the crowd I ran with shared my interest, and so I kept it to myself, releasing it only when I would sneak to a dirty bookshop and buy a gay S&M magazine.

II. When I was 18 and 19, I had a lover. We were romantic and mushy, always dating and making sweet love. It was good— very good—but for me there was always the sense of something missing, something hard and masculine that I craved.

Eventually we broke up, and I sank into a private, celibate world of masturbation and S&M magazines. I grew fat and intellectual, ignoring myself in an orgy of neglect and self-loathing.

III. This period of celibacy ended abruptly one spring, when I drove to San Francisco and hired the services of two male prostitutes. The manner in which they took me—rough and demanding—satisfied me as never before, but the experience left me hungry for more.

IV. Two years later I moved to a large city near San Francisco, and it was then that I began what I now refer to as my "experimentations" in sadomasochism, or more precisely, in masochism. Through a friend I met a man who was himself a slave. He and I had one sex session, in which he demonstrated all sorts of sexual devices and proceeded to spank me with a belt. He jerked me off with an oiled piece of leather, surely one of the most exquisite sensations my cock had ever known.

What followed was a year of dabbling, a number of frustrated connections with other men, who, like myself, were looking for a rough scene. But I could never find what I was looking for—a certain combination of sex as a bottom and a sort of hoped-for degradation, or possession, perhaps objectification.

V. My experimentations gained me a certain degree of experience. I learned to have my ass reddened with a belt and leather strap. I learned to endure (and enjoy) lengthy periods of bondage. I began to suspect, in an intellectual way, that sadomasochism was an extremely advanced form of sex, in which humans called upon their special capacities to think and imagine—rather than simply rutting as nature dictated.

Yet something was missing, some immediacy, some essence of suddenness or surprise. I began to understand that I was not interested in "light" S&M. I was seeking a heavier scene; I wanted slave training.

VI. I moved to San Francisco and bought leathers—jacket, boots, chaps. These gave me the appearance I needed, but the black leather remained an adornment, not a symbol, not a statement of who I really was, or really, who I wanted to be.

I wanted to be a slave. I wanted to be ordered to strip, to kneel before one or two hunky men with big cocks, to suck their dicks and eat their asses. I wanted to be tied up, immobile, to be beaten, whipped, spit on, pissed on. I wanted to be fucked violently. I wanted my tits pinched hard, my balls squeezed and tortured. I wanted to crawl around the floor dragging weights from my tits and balls.

I wanted to live out the scenes I had read about and seen in the porno books, mags, and films.

VII. And then, one evening, in a sudden and shocking realization, I remembered my boyhood friend Bob, who had played with me in violent and sexual ways when we were not more than seven or eight years old.

When I remembered this, I was amazed that I had ever forgotten those afternoons after school, when he and I would play "prison camps." He would lock me in their basement and order me to be naked by the time he returned. But I could never strip in time, and so I'd have to finish stripping while he watched, then suffer "punishment" for failing to undress quickly enough.

Later, I'd repeat the same punishment on another neighborhood boy, delighting in his pain when I'd hit his balls as hard as I could. Had the seed been planted that eventually grew into my manhood desires?

VIII. After discovering my talents as a bottom in San Francisco's baths and sex clubs, the frustration overwhelmed me, and I made an intellectual decision to involve myself in masochism. The only way I knew to do this was to hire a Master, so I carefully chose a "model" from the pink section of the ADVOCATE, made a date, and withdrew the requisite hundred dollars from my savings account.

IX. Master Daniel opened the door and invited me in. He questioned my experience, discovered certain of my fantasies, and then ordered me to strip at once. He led me to a sex chamber, all panelled in mirrors, the walls displaying an extensive collection of sexual devices—whips, ropes, dildoes.

He brought a leather harness and placed it on my body, fitting my balls and already hard cock snugly into a steel cockring fitted into the harness. He then stripped down to a leather jockstrap and boots and ordered me to kneel and lick his boots.

I began, eager to please this man, this first real master. He told me to work my tongue up the inside of his legs, and I did so, licking and caressing the firm muscles there with my hot tongue. When I reached the leather jockstrap—which was now bulging with his huge prick—I stopped short. Was a slave supposed to continue? Should I take the initiative and lick that mound?

Apparently my hesitation pleased him, for he patted me on the head and then told me to go ahead and feast my tongue on the leather pouch. I began to lick the leather, to spit-shine it good. I had read enough pornography and had entertained enough fantasies to know that this was just the beginning.

And I was right. What he did next was let free his huge dick, but he told me only to look at it, to appreciate its masterful beauty. Then he ordered me to stand, to lay myself on my back in the leather sling.

I did so, and he tied my ankles securely to the chains supporting the suspended sling, then tied my wrists to the chains above my head. Next he took a leather hood with eye slits and an opening at the mouth, and slid it over my head.

The sensation of the hood on my head was strange, foreign, and undeniably erotic. Something happened when that leather hood covered my face. Somehow I became another person, someone totally outside myself, and I felt an odd, exhilarating sense of freedom. The sexual urges welled up within me, and he recognized that the hood had had a profound effect on me, on my fantasy about what was taking place.

Next began the whipping. At first it was gentle, slow, very teasing, but as my butt warmed to the whip, I squirmed around and down, begging physically for more of the belt. And he let me have it. I had never imagined that I could endure such severe flogging, but something in my mind snapped, something gave way, and suddenly the line was crossed—the pain and the sting of the whip translated itself into an exquisite, overwhelming pleasure. I had read about that line between pain and pleasure, and in that moment I experienced it.

As quickly as the beating began, it stopped. My field of vision was restricted by the small eye openings in the hood, so for a few moments my master was lost from sight. I relaxed into the sling, discovering that I had tensed nearly every muscle in my arms and legs during the flogging.

The next thing I felt was a burning pain in my tits. It felt as though my tits were being seared, and I spoke out: "Master, no, it's too much . . ." But just as I was complaining, his mouth covered mine, his loving tongue probing deeply into my mouth, and again—though much more intensely—the line was crossed, and the pain of the tight steel tit clamps was translated into indescribable pleasure. The isolated, perfect sensation was exquisite, almost Oriental in its simplicity and focus. But then, slowly but in a rush, the sensation translated itself into a furious warm rush coursing through my body, emanating outward from my nipples like rays of light.

My master pulled his mouth away and positioned himself at the end of the sling, between my legs. I felt the head of his cock pressed against my asshole, felt a glob of lube smeared onto my hungry hole, and then with great dexterity and certainty he slid his whole throbbing cock inside me, in one long, sure movement.

I had never taken a cock so easily, so simply, but his expertise in sex was undeniable. He took me fast and hard, ramming again and again into my writhing ass, holding onto my balls tightly with his hand, while slapping my raw butt with the other hand.

He came fast, too soon almost. I felt hollow, as though the experience had been cut short, but then I felt his mouth slide down over my dick, sucking it into his throat and juicing it for its load. He didn't have to work long, for I was brought to orgasm in a matter of seconds.

And when I came, his hands deftly flew over my body, releasing the tit clamps, pulling off the hood—all in a swift motion of release that coincided with the instant of my enormous ejaculation. As quickly as he accomplished this, he untied my ankles, untied my wrists, unhooked the body harness, and I was free, completely unfettered, completely spent. The orgasm had been a vast, wild liberation.

I raised my head and looked into his smiling face. He was pleased. I whispered: "I love you."

X. The scene was finished, it was done. I had done it; I had realized my most compelling fantasy, had met my deepest need. I was amazed, though, at the goodness of it all. It was not dark and sinister or foreboding. Two men had come together in a mutual, deeply satisfying connection, and my surprise—and delight—at the outcome overwhelmed me for a time.

My fears and curiosities had vanished. It was not dangerous. It was not physically damaging. It was not painful. What should have been pain had crossed over into perfect pleasure. I was not psychologically wrecked; I was fulfilled. My masculinity was affirmed—wildly so—in the blatant show of strength, endurance, and privately shared male pleasure. The experience was nothing short of profound.

XI. When I left that night, I felt I had finally found what I had been wanting for so many years, all my life it seemed. Just before I had gone, Master Daniel invited me to be his slave, his personal slave, forget the money. Without hesitation I agreed, and since that first meeting I have become his sex slave, to use as he pleases, without question.

But it is not at all how one might imagine. My masochism does not preclude my romantic entanglements with others, nor does it infringe on my habitual and satisfying raunchy sex life at the baths and clubs. It is a completely different way of making love. There is nothing like it.

DIARY OF A SADIST

I RECENTLY SAW A T-SHIRT in San Francisco that had written across the front: *It takes a good bottom to get to the top.* Although somewhat ambiguous, the phrase—as I interpret it—reveals a bit of truth. To be a good topman, you've got to learn the ropes as a bottom man.

It was as a result of my years of training and experience as a masochist that I developed my sense of sexual sadism. It was nothing sudden, nothing angry. Rather, it was a gradual recognition that masochism and sadism are really the same thing, that both urges are rooted in the same impulse of sexual aggression. They differ only insofar as the expression of that impulse is concerned. When the aggression is directed outward—onto another person—it is sadism. When it is directed inward—onto oneself—it is masochism.

Now it is important to note here that I make no judgements, place no values on the respective roles: I do not consider sadomasochism perverted nor an expression of misanthropy. And I do not feel that a masochist is secretly trying to destroy himself, anymore than I feel that a sadist is out to get somebody's blood. It really is a matter of how one gets one's kicks.

It was over dinner with a friend that the notion of myself as a sadist was first entertained. This man had been very experienced in sadomasochism, and he suggested that I did not really know myself, that I was misinterpreting my own desires when I said that I was a bottom, a masochist.

I could find no reason why he should make such an observation. He pointed out that in all the other areas of my life I was a topman: at home, on the job, in my career, in my dealings with other people. I was always in control of the situations around me; and for this reason he felt that, in the sexual arena, I would surely seek to control.

As a good slave I was in control, I told him; it was the bottom who was always in control of the situation. He agreed with this, but he pointed out that it was not necessarily one who led so much as symbolically controlled—who held the keys to the kingdom, so to speak.

Perhaps he was right. Perhaps I did want to control the sexual scenario as much as possible. Perhaps by assuming the role as topman, as sadist, I would find even greater satisfaction.

Nothing came of this discussion of my sex life for many months. I remained a good slave, seeking new masters, turning my bottom up at the clubs and savoring the attentions of topmen who needed a good and willing bottom to rough up, to fuck good and hard, to service them as they saw fit.

But a gradual shift was beginning. Over a period of several months, I found it more and more difficult to acquire a topman for the night. I would offer myself in the usual ways and no one was taking. I would even emphasize my slavery with a collar or leather armband wrapped around my right bicep, yet the topmen would pass me by—often for others less attractive, less willing, less evident as slaves. It was nothing to do with my looks or costuming.

After this purgatory of neutrality, a period followed wherein I was approached by bottom men. More and more frequently slaves, and other submissives, would present themselves to me at the clubs or even on the street, offer themselves for my pleasure.

I simply ignored them and wondered how they could be so stupid as to not see that I, too, was a bottom. Then I decided to try it.

I was standing in line on Castro Street in San Francisco, at the donut shop near the corner of 18th Street. I was cold, damp from the fog or rain or whatever the hell that is in San Francisco. As I stood there, I noticed a young man beside me, hunky, handsome, definitely interested in the bulge that is always present in my jeans.

"Pretty cold out, isn't it?" he asked.

"And wet," I said, noticing with great interest that his ass was very small, round, and looked hard.

"Bet you could show me something to warm me up," was his propositional line. Although I seriously debated if I could carry on with someone who opened with a line like that, that firm round ass was making me very horny.

He told me that there was no need to stand in line any further; he could find us something to eat at his place just up the street. So we walked up Castro Street to his apartment above some stores. When we got inside, I realized that I was feeling very hot, very heavy, and very sadistic. For some reason, I wanted to use this guy the way men always used me; and there was no desire on my part to be used by him. I wanted to top him.

As we began that evening, I realized quickly I had to confront many issues within my own sadomasochistic sexuality. I began to feel a sense of male power, as I began to top this young man, of something macho and aggressive that was unlike the passion I had always experienced as a bottom. There was something almost foreign about it, and it took me a moment to realize what it was.

Now I no longer consider this to be a factor, but at that moment—as I was about to enter into the sexual experience as a master—I suddenly felt very strongly identified with, of all things, straight men. I was about to dominate—not to yield, not to really give up anything to anyone else—but to take, to seize, and to use.

This was a frightening realization for two reasons. I felt a horror that I was somehow affirming the enemy (heterosexual males) by engaging in their most cherished activity (strictly fucking, possessing); this notion passed when I realized that the object of my affections was still a boy, not a girl, and this kept the enemy at bay. The second part of the fright was a sudden

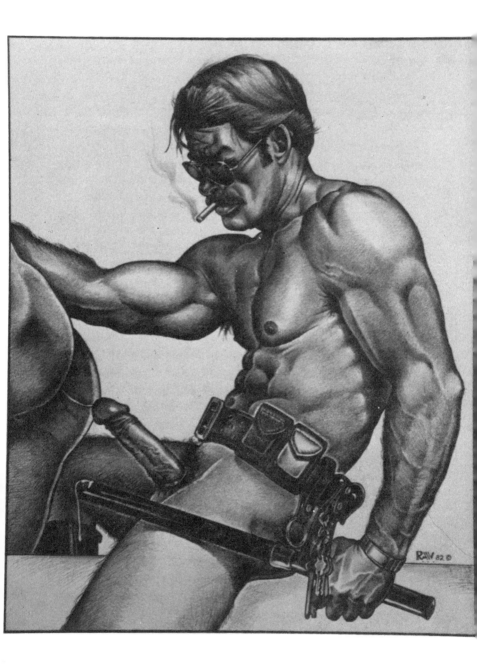

recognition within myself that I was fully a man just like those heterosexual possessors; my urge to take and use this young bottom-man originated in the same place as the urge in the heterosexual man. Only the instrument of my satisfaction—the object—was changed.

Well, once I had ordered the man to strip and kneel, and once I had seen the magnificence of well-toned body and generous sexual equipment, I had no qualms about seizing this as my own, at least for the time being.

As he knelt before me on the floor, I began by tying his hands together behind his back. His servile position, and the vulnerability of his genitals and ass, were a real turn on for me as a new topman: mine to do with as I pleased. I slowly felt him all over, running my hands over his nipples, squeezing his balls, pulling on his thickening cock—he had a surprisingly huge dick. My mind was flooded with possibilities as I toyed with this young slave, fully conscious that I could do whatever I liked with him.

But as I brought him to his feet and reached around to play with his ass, to probe the tight hole where I would eventually place my hard-on, I was filled with a deep sense of responsibility. The scenario was being left in my hands, in my imagination, and although I knew (from my own experience) what he wanted, the burden of creating it and providing it for him was very heavy.

It was also stimulating. I was the potent force in the room, the deciding factor, the man in charge of his body and pleasure. It thrilled me to twist his nipples and see him writhe in exquisite pleasure, thrilled me to grab hold of his big balls and yank, sending waves of pain-pleasure through his body, to shove my greasy fingers into his butt and pry it open for the invasion of big cock.

I bent him over the edge of the table and striped his ass with my belt. I had never whipped before, so this experience was a strange—and gratifying—one. To see the cheeks of his ass redden and his hips rotate to meet the blows was like looking into a mirror of my own passion as a whipping boy. To give such satisfactory painful pleasure to another man, by inflicting my aggressions on him in a semi-brutal manner, intoxicated me; I was intoxicated with masculinity, potency, with power over another man.

When his ass was hot, I discarded the belt and positioned myself behind him, looking down at the round, red ass, the tight greasy hole waiting for a big prick to open it up. I ran my hands over the flesh, tested the sphincter, then began to probe the tight opening with the head of my aching flesh.

I stuck in just the head of my dick, and then pulled it out again. I made him ask me. I made him shout it out—I had a man begging me to stick my dick up his butt!

And so I did. Sank the whole eight inches in up to my balls, revelling in his body writhing beneath me, twisting and turning to absorb as much of a topman's virility as he could. Then, I fucked him, as hard and fast as I wanted, experiencing a new sensation of prevalence and power. I held onto his bound wrists for support and bucked my hips forward, ramming my dick, impaling that red-hot ass.

He begged for more. And I complied. I fucked him and then fucked him some more, in every position I could imagine, tugging on his tits til they bruised, grabbing onto his balls til he begged for me to cum.

I did cum. And then, while he was still working his butt to suck as much of my squirting dick inside him as he could, I bent down to his stiff thick meat and sucked him off. He shot so much I thought I'd choke, but the sensation was wonderful— bringing this little hunk to orgasm after vilely abusing him for my own pleasure (and his, of course).

This one isolated experience did not create my whole persona as a topman, but it was the first full physical expression of that urge which had been left un-explored all my life.

I did not abandon my activities as a slave, but I did begin to master others, to top when the time and context were right. And I have never doubted my identity as a topman as well as a bottom-man, since that night.

I am mystified by my versatility at times, but as the t-shirt in San Francisco said: *It takes a good bottom to get to the top.*

WE MEAT AGAIN

I NEVER THOUGHT THAT ANYTHING would come of our chance meeting in front of Macy's that day. After all, I hadn't seen Trent for over two years, and although I enjoyed running into him like that, I assumed that was it—just a chance encounter on the street, nothing more.

But then I saw him again, this time at a cafe in Chelsea, and I began to wonder if maybe it might be fun to rekindle the old flame, get together again. I walked over to his booth and said hi, asked if we could chat.

"Of course," he answered, "we really should have gotten together the other day when we met at Macy's." And so we began to catch up on ourselves over the past couple of years. His business was flourishing, and I was doing pretty well in my own line of consulting. But my sex life had gotten unusually dull, the result of my own timidity in strange times; the prospect of getting together again with Trent—strong, firm, healthy— made me feel some of the old edge I used to feel.

He talked about his business—he did lighting installations— and I watched his mouth form itself around the words, his lips a soft natural pink, curving gently beneath the bushy black moustache. Every once in a while his tongue would flick out to wet his lower lip, and I could already imagine how it would feel to have that warm red tongue flicker across the head of my dick again.

He raised his hand and toyed with the end of his moustache. I watched his long, strong fingers twist the tiny black hairs. My eyes wandered down his thick neck to the round, muscular shoulders which seemed to run in one thick piece into his hard chest. His shirt was unbuttoned halfway down his torso, and I could see the firm outline of his chest muscles—naturally firm and defined, not gym creations. Soft, curly black hair shadowed the valley between his pecs.

He moved in his chair and I glanced down at his thighs, packed tight in a pair of jeans, and his narrow waist encircled by a thick leather belt. God, did he have charisma! His thighs stretched against the denim; he extended his long legs languorously, expectantly, yet somehow they remained indifferent.

I could just imagine myself poised over his hard, yielding body, his long legs stretched out and raised high. I could almost feel the head of my hard dick pressed against that soft pink hole, knowing that in just a moment the full length of my cock would slide inside him.

I broke my reverie and asked him to come home with me, right then; to my happy surprise he was agreeable: "I wondered when you'd get around to asking. Let's go." And so we gathered our things and made our way out the door. We decided to walk, it wasn't far, and as we started down the street I made an effort to trail behind him for a moment, so that I could see his round firm ass in his jeans, swaying ever so slightly, hinting at the pleasure to come.

Trent walked on ahead, aware that his ass was the object of my scrutiny. He swayed a bit—once—and then returned to his usual masculine swagger. But he knew it had been enough. He was glad; he wanted his legs wrapped around his man, spread open to take thick meat inside. He wanted mouths glued together, tongues probing, playing.

I came alongside him once again and we walked on. Our earlier romance—two years ago—had been tumultuous, with more arguing than love-making, more cancelled dates than nights together in bed. And so this moment—as we strolled towards my apartment and contemplated the night to come—

this moment was full of excitement, sexual tension, a wonderful, hopeful expectancy.

We got to my building and climbed the stairs. I opened the door to my place, a good-sized flat decorated mostly in "bachelor." He kicked off his boots and went into the kitchen, almost too familiarly, and made himself a Tom Collins, with lime, not lemon, as always.

He came back into the living room where I was hanging up my jacket, and collapsed lazily into the big overstuffed couch. "Always loved this couch," he said, sinking into the cushions and spreading his legs comfortably. I sat beside him, taking a sip of the Collins, letting my hand come to rest on his thigh. I could see the outline of his cock through the denim, the generous bulge of his nuts.

"Yes," he said simply, still sipping his drink and then slipping one of his hands over mine. He took my hand and moved it slowly up his thigh, towards his crotch. Instantly I began to stiffen in my trousers, my swelling dick betraying my emotions.

His hand guided me tightly between his legs, over the bulges and down to the warmth of his ass. Without saying a word I began to rub my hand against that warmth behind his balls. He sipped his drink, leaned back and closed his eyes. His lips parted slightly with an almost imperceptible sigh.

I couldn't stand the suspense, I never could. I kept on rubbing my hand between his legs, feeling the warmth of his ass beneath the denim. He leaned back further, scooted his ass forward, parted his legs further so that I could knead the spot between them. I felt the heat rising there, even felt a mild dampness. We had to get naked, soon.

To see him, this big hunk of a handsome guy, lying there with his legs spread and my hand rubbing between them, waiting, giving; to have so much man—so much muscle, so much dick, so much balls, so much kindness and toughness and vulnerability all wrapped up together in this hot man—to have him offering himself to me was a heady, explosive pleasure.

As one hand masturbated his ass and balls through the jeans, I brought the other hand up to his shirt and let my fingers caress his chest. He arched himself towards me, pushing his muscular chest forward for me to fondle. I ran my hand over the shirt, then under, feeling and squeezing his full chest. Then, lightly, I pinched the nipples, watching the sensation send him into ecstasy.

I unbuttoned the shirt, revelling in the sight that unfolded before my eyes. I pulled the material away, yanked it out of his jeans, and let my eyes feast on the luscious curves of muscle, the dark pink nipples standing up erect; ready to be touched, sucked, tugged.

I continued to strip him, unfastening his jeans and pulling them down around his hips. He lifted himself up so that the jeans slipped off his hips. His cock and balls sprang free, bouncing and rising in the air. His groin was the vortex of his body's perfection: the fuzzy dark hair planted around the thick trunk of his cock, the heavy ball sac hanging low, the soft, pink spot where I would slide my aching dick.

It needed release, too. I stripped off my clothes—with his help. He whispered that he loved stripping me, and so I sat back, letting his fingers fumble with buttons and buckle and zipper. As he moved, stripping me naked, I watched his long cock sway in the air, watched his low-hanging balls flop between his legs, watched as he got on his knees and spread his legs slightly when he tugged on the legs of my trousers to pull them off. I stared at the way his cock swayed as he moved; it was eight inches, and it jutted straight out, its weight causing it to sway heavily.

We were both naked now. My cock throbbed against my belly as his fist closed around it and stroked lightly, teasingly. I wanted nothing more than to dive between his legs with my tongue, to find that tender spot behind his balls and drive him into a state of wild readiness, then plunge my big dick inside his wet hole and fuck him till we both shrieked in pleasure.

And so I leaned down between his legs, smelled the sexy mustiness of his crotch, a smell that always makes me crazy to eat dick. I moved my tongue over his ball sac, then along the underside of his towering meat. He lay back on the couch and spread his legs wide, letting his feet come to rest on my back. My tongue worked in ovals along the inside of his thighs, then his balls, then his dick. As I sucked and slurped on his fat dick, feeling it slide deep into my throat, I stuck a finger in his asshole, delighting in the moan he made, delighting in the warm dampness and slickness of his hole, which was already wet with desire.

Without hesitation I brought myself full length on top of him, lowered my body on top of his. Our arms wrapped us together, our lips met, then parted at once to give way to the probing tongues, mine tasting of cock and balls.

I felt my cock pressed along his belly, felt his big piece thrust against my thigh. I started to hump him, rubbing my dick along his flat hairy stomach. He reached between us, found my nipples, and pinched them lightly between his fingers. Then his tongue found them, and he sucked and nibbled my tits. I thought my cock might burst with the vast pleasure, but then he spread his legs wide, wrapped them behind my back, and with a deft motion of his hips brought my erection into line with his damp asshole.

"Fuck me," he said. "Shove your dick inside me and fuck the shit out of me." He whispered heavily in my ear, his voice husky and deep with lust.

"Okay, baby," was all I said as the head of my hard-on pressed against the round, tight hole, probed the opening of the passage. I smeared it with the heavy flow of my slick pre-cum. I let the head of my cock press against his hole for a moment, gently prying the tight muscular ring open an inch or so. Then, when he arched his back and tried to force me to enter him, I pulled back ever so slightly.

"Please," he said, raising his hips again.

"Okay, you got it," I said, finally letting my huge cock slide inside him. He gasped and clawed at my back as the long dick rammed him unexpectedly hard. His hips raised, and our bellies met — his cock between them — in a fusion of sudden possession.

As I rammed my hard-on in and out of his tight hole, it was like being grasped by a strong hand and then gently caressed; he knew how to use his asshole. First it would tighten around my pounding tool, then loosen and almost ripple over it. I experienced unimagined pleasure as my erection rammed into him again and again.

His hips rotated rhythmically to meet my hard thrusts, his tongue claimed my mouth hungrily, his fingers tore into my nipples, my hands clawed at his hair, his tits, his muscles. We grew ferocious and sweaty; we left behind all semblance of gentility in the mad pounding of our bodies. I was drunk on lust—I must drive this hard man into a frenzy.

"Yeah," he said, his hips moving demandingly. He tried to suck as much of my huge cock inside him as he could. "Take me, babe, fuck me, shoot your hot cum inside my ass."

I rammed my sextool deep and hard, knowing that very soon my cum would squirt out. My balls tightened; he reached around and grabbed them, squeezed them hard, tugging roughly.

Then, as he yanked on my balls, and as I shoved my cock as deep and hard as I could, I felt his whole body tense, felt him tighten his grasp on my captive nuts. And then he was writhing beneath me, his ass grabbing and rippling over my turgid cock. His enormous dick rammed against my belly, then his orgasm shook him violently, tremendous gobs of hot white jism squirted out and covered our bellies with cum.

Just as his dick squirted its hot load, I felt the cum churning in my balls, felt the sudden surge of power and release as the hot liquid shot up the length of my dick and emptied in huge spurts into his ass. It seemed I would never stop coming as I pumped more and more of the hot load inside him.

But then it was over. We were lying beside each other, our lips touching, our tongues lightly playing. My hands rested on his chest, his hands cupped my nuts and encircled my bloated dick.

"I'm glad we ran into each other," he said simply.

I agreed. I said that perhaps we should try to get together again. Again. But he said no, let's not do that scene again. I knew what he meant. And so we rested content in our chance encounter.

CLUB MAVERICK

R ICK HAD BEEN AROUND. He'd been in love, out of love, had long love affairs, brief romances, cruised the park scene, sucked dick in a public bathroom, made love in the woods, in the car, even in the back of church. He'd been to the baths and the bars, tasted the high-paced scene of the discos and backrooms.

For the past few years, though, he'd noticed that the bar scene was changing, that the backrooms were all gone, that bars were places to have a drink, maybe dance a little, but not places for finding easy sex. The baths had changed, too, as far as he could tell. Used to be that an evening at the baths was a hot affair, picking and choosing which hunky stud might invite him to his little room. But now the baths were populated by pretty boys and men that were so picky they probably never got it on.

Rick had traveled around a bit, too, the last few years, checking out New York, Chicago, Key West, and L.A. Now he lived in San Francisco. He found that it lived up to its reputation as a wild town. There were beautiful hunky studs everywhere, all of them ready, willing, and able, as they say. He was especially attracted to the leather scene in San Francisco's Folsom district. Those studs knew what they wanted—hard sex and lots of it.

For some reason, though, Rick had avoided the whole province of the leather set known as the "clubs." Many of his friends got their sex regularly at the clubs, but he had never tried it.

He usually went out to one of the great leather or western bars, had a few drinks, and then would go home with a leather dude and get into the raunchy mansex in private.

Rick knew that he wanted to go to a club. He knew that the clubs in San Francisco were some of the best, ranking right up there with New York and Berlin. The only thing that held him back was that he wasn't entirely sure what to expect, didn't have much confidence that he knew the protocol of cruising behavior in a sex club.

Finally, though, Rick was ready. It was a Friday night, he'd had a few drinks with a friend at the Eagle, and he was horny, damn horny. He asked his friend about the clubs.

"Well," his friend said, "there's a whole bunch you could try. Some of 'em are pretty heavy, though, and some of 'em just don't suit me at all. What do you want to do?"

"Fuck," Rick answered with a laugh.

"Shit, I know that, asshole," his friend said. "I mean, do you want to get into piss, or scat, or do you want to take acid and roam some darkened hallways looking at naked slaves in bondage?"

"Jesus fucking Christ!" Rick said, "It sounds like a goddamn smorgasbord!"

"It is, man, believe me. So what is it?"

"Well, you know my scene," Rick answered. "I like some pretty heavy stuff. I like getting naked and getting tied up and fucked. I like getting pissed on, but I don't drink it."

His friend swallowed his beer and asked the bartender for another. Loud music pounded in the bar, making it hard for the two to carry on the conversation. His friend got the beer and turned to Rick and said:

"The Caldron is the place for you."

"The Caldron? Sounds sinister . . ."

"Oh, it ain't scary, man; it's just super hard-core, man-sized sex, and plenty of it, too."

"Well," Rick said, "what's it like? I mean, how do you do it, get in, and all?"

"It's just like a bath only different. First, it's a private club, so you've got to buy a membership for a few dollars, then you pay an admission for the evening. When you get inside you can do whatever you like. There's a clothes check, a place to douche, you know. It's pretty good, too, probably the best in San Francisco."

"How big is it?" Rick asked.

"Really big, a lot bigger than most places. I guess it's the closest thing San Francisco has to the Mineshaft in New York City."

"Sounds hot," Rick said. His cock was bulging in his jeans just thinking about going to this place, a big building full of hunky dudes devoted to one thing: heavy sex. Rick got the directions on how to get there. They finished their beer, watching the bar crowd start to thin. It was close to last call, and the leathermen were starting to leave in pairs, or threes, maybe two masters with a slave following behind, headed for a night of obedience and sex. Many left alone, climbing on their motorcycles or into their pickups and heading for the clubs, horny as hell and ready to fuck.

Rick finished his beer and said goodbye to his friend. He was ready to try it out, so he left the bar, walked over to 11th Street and began to walk towards the Caldron. It was a warm spring evening, something rare in San Francisco, and there were a lot of leathermen out on Folsom Street. Rick waited at the corner for the light to change, watching the hot studs cruise by on their motorcycles, proclaiming their dominance by wearing keys or leather arm bands on the left.

Rick knew the leather scene fairly well, but in many ways he was still a novice. He had been trained to serve one or two masters, had learned to enjoy bondage for great lengths of time. But the part that excited him, that virtually addicted him to the leather set, was not the flashy accoutrements of keys or armbands or images made by leather chaps, body harnesses, or handcuffs. No, these were the symbols of the real thing, the real sexual communication going on, call it love if you want.

The real thing about hardsex, leathersex, B&D, S&M, whatever, was in the willingness to help another man create and live out his fantasy. It involved an incredible amount of communication, sharing, planning. But most of all, it involved caring. To participate in an extremely advanced form of sex showed a great willingness to contribute oneself to a larger reality, to the reality of being a man among men, the reality of pure masculinity, the reality of having sex the way all men really want to have sex. That's why Rick called it "mansex," and that's why he was drawn to remain one of the leather crowd. The leather set was into mansex.

Rick crossed Folsom as the light turned green. A motorcycle sped past him, only a couple feet away as the stud raced through the red light. Rick had to laugh at the attitude, and he nodded at the rider, acknowledging his assertion of power. This is fine, Rick thought as he walked up 11th Street, this is damn fine.

He thought some more about mansex, hoping that the Caldron turned out to be everything he was expecting. From his friend's description, this should be a very important night for Rick. A maverick, he thought, that's what I am, a greenhorn, a club maverick. Rick had to laugh at the idea of himself as new to anything, as being virginal to any experience. But here he was, on a Friday night in May, crossing Howard Street and approaching the little alley that led to the Caldron.

He rounded the corner at the little alley, walked to the middle of the block, turned and found the Caldron. He was surprised to see a line of men waiting to get in, but realized what a good sign that was. He sized up the guys in line. They were all, every one of them, really hunky men. Muscles bulged and rippled, leather creaked, sweat glistened on bared chests.

The line moved quickly and Rick finally found himself at the window, explaining that he'd like to buy a membership. The man at the window was just a hint of what was inside. Rick was shocked and pleased to see that the guy wore a soaked jockstrap and a torn t-shirt. He was a small, muscular man with a black beard. His naked ass looked delicious, Rick thought when the guy turned around to get Rick's new membership card. He handed it to Rick and smiled wryly as he buzzed Rick through the black door into the interior of the Caldron.

Rick wasn't prepared for what he saw. Scores of muscular studs stood around drinking and laughing in what was obviously just the front section of a huge, cavernous building. There was a large bar, and as Rick looked at the men standing around it, he was surprised to see several men chatting amiably with friends while nude guys sucked on their dicks or ate their asses. Two or three guys were getting fucked at the bar, big cocks pumping in and out of their asses while they drank a beer, talked with friends. It was the most relaxed, yet sexually intense thing Rick had ever seen. The sexual tension was high; these men were serious about their fun, yet their laughter and good times betrayed a genuine lightness, as though their forthright assertion of their desires set them free from any nonsense role playing, from any dark sinister nonsense that had nothing to do with being a good top or a good bottom or having good rough sex.

Rick liked it at once. He felt at home there. He did another sweep of the bar with his eyes, then walked to the clothes check room directly in front of him down a dark hall. He checked his leather jacket and shirt, stripped down to his jeans and boots. Next he knew he'd have to take a look around to get the lay of the land.

The place seemed endless. One big room opened into yet another big room, each offering some sort of equipment for various kinds of sex. There were slings and tables and even an old surgeon's table. The place was dimly lit by red and orange lights, casting a hellish glow on the naked bodies pressed together, weaving complex patterns of movement. The center of the place was a huge open space with four slings arranged beneath bright white lights. The slings were occupied by sweaty studs with fists shoved up their asses. The fist fuckers were lost in their own private world of intense pleasure, and Rick moved on to another section of the club.

There was a big wooden table lit from above by a dull orange light. There was a can of grease in the center of the table, and several men stood around the table, stroking their long hardons and watching a man at the end of the table who had his dick up one guy's ass, and his two fists up two other guys' asses. Rick pulled his own thick tool out of his jeans and began to pull on his dick. The fucker had huge muscular arms, a hairy chest, and he wore black leather chaps as he pumped his cock and fists into the three men bent over the table. Their hard round asses glowed in the orange light, moving gently to the rhythm of the plowing dick and fists. Rick watched as the leatherman came close to shooting his load, saw how hard he rammed his dick into the greasy hole and pumped his arms into the two assholes. When the dude shot his cum into the little stud in the center, he let out a loud moan, and a couple of the guys standing around the table shot their hot jism all over the wet tabletop.

Rick walked into the next room, leaving his big bloated dick hanging out the front of his jeans. Everyone else seemed to let their dicks hang free, or else they were completely naked, so he figured he'd join them.

He walked into a big square room with a low leather platform in the center. There were many men around the periphery of the room getting fucked up against the wall, or sucked off, or kissing passionately. On the platform lay a slave in bondage. He was being worked over heavily by two leather-clad masters, submitting to their orders as the other men in the room looked on.

The slave wore a dog collar, to which was attached a chain that led to his bound wrists. A long chain bound his legs together, and at the moment his face was obscured by one of the masters, who was sitting on the slave's tongue, ordered him to eat his ass. The other master was involved in some sort of genitorture, alternately squeezing and tugging on the slave's big balls and huge curving tool.

Rick found the whole scene super horny. He knew it couldn't be long before he'd have to get into something himself; the pressure was already beginning to build up in his nuts. His exposed dick was hanging heavy, half pumped up and dripping thick pre-cum juice. He decided to check out the last room, way up in the front, then he'd look for some real action.

The room in the front was the best Rick found. In the center of the room were two free-standing porcelain tubs, surrounded by hunky studs all pissing on the dudes lying in the tubs. At the far end of the room was a small bathroom; there was a young guy sitting on the toilet drinking piss from the buff dudes lined up to take a leak. The guy wore a wet athletic shirt that had the word "urinal" printed on the front.

More men stood around the walls, drinking beer and pulling on their dicks. Occasionally one of them would kneel down in front of a muscular dude and drink the dude's piss. Rick stood up against the wall for a few minutes, surveying the hot scene around him.

As he stood there, a tall handsome man with a dark moustache came and stood beside him. He was drinking a beer and gently caressing his fat prick. Rick looked him up and down, appraising the fine muscles and feeling his own dick start to lengthen. He knew what to do, and it was late enough, he was horny enough, and he'd had enough to drink. He stepped out, stood in front of the handsome man, and knelt down.

At once the long fat dick in his face erupted a hot stream of beer piss, clear and salty, flooding Rick's mouth, running down his chin, soaking his jeans and moustache. He swallowed some of the piss, and let some of it spill out of his mouth, splashing onto his hard manmeat.

"Yeah, man, drink that piss," the dude said, pouring some of his cold beer onto Rick's head and back. Rick gobbled at the big dick hungrily, sucking the hot liquid from the throbbing fountain.

When the man stopped pissing, another muscular guy came up and started to piss on Rick. Rick felt the hot spray hit his shoulder first, then the guy aimed the piss at his chest, directing his dick like a firehose, spraying burning urine all over Rick's kneeling body. Rick stroked his raging sextool, jerking himself faster and harder, feeling the cum boiling in his nuts. The piss poured into his mouth. For a moment he flashed on his statement earlier in the evening that he "didn't drink piss," and for a split second he wondered how he had crossed the limit so easily, but then the last of the piss squirted into his thirsty mouth and hisown hot cum shot up out of his pulsing tool, squirting and pumping high into the air, onto the hairy legs of the stud pissing on him, coating his own hand with slippery jism. And then it was done, he was drenched, his dick dripped cum, his mouth dripped warm urine.

The two guys helped him stand, patted him on the back. "That was fuckin' good!" the second guy said, slapping Rick on the ass. "You're a hot guy."

"Yeah, it was," Rick agreed, putting his hand around the back of the man's neck and rubbing it.

"How 'bout a beer up front?" the man invited.

"Okay, sounds fine," Rick said, adjusting his wet jeans and stuffing his slick cock back inside. "I think I could use drying off."

"Don't worry about it," the guy said, introducing himself as Steve.

They went up front to the bar. Steve gave two tokens to the bartender, who handed him two tall beers. They took seats at the bar, enjoying the glances from the other studs who recognized what must have just gone down.

"So, what's your name?" Steve asked.

"Oh, sorry," Rick apologized, "I'm Rick. This is my first time here . . . or any club really."

"Are you shittin' me?" Steve asked incredulously.

"Hell no, man, I'm for real," Rick answered. "A friend told me about this place, and I had to check it out."

"Alright! I'm glad you did, you're a good piss-drinker."

"Well, that was a first for me too."

"Naw . . ."

"I mean, I been pissed *on* before, but I've never swallowed it," Rick admitted.

"It's nothing, man, just piss," Steve said, taking a long swig off his beer.

"I know, I was surprised at how fuckin' hot it was."

"So," Steve said, looking at Rick closely, "sounds like you're pretty new to things."

"Well, not so new as you'd think," Rick said. "I mean, I've done plenty; I've had some slave training . . ."

"Yeah?" Steve broke in.

"Yeah, some slave training, and I'm a good bottom, not bad as a top either. I don't know, it's just that for all I've done in the past, it seems like lately there's a kind of opening-up process going on, some kind of relaxation or maybe a loss of fear that lets me go ahead and explore my fantasies, find out what they're about, and sometimes, then, you know, to live them."

"I know what you mean," Steve said. "I did the same thing a few years ago when this whole scene started to flourish. I had a lover at the time, and he did something that just opened my whole world. It was more than sex, a lot more. It just let me open up and look inside, to find out what it is to be a man, what it is to be macho, and what it's like to have sex with men the way we want to do it."

"God, I was thinking the same thing a while ago, when I was walking up here, about how my sex fantasies are the way men are, the way we like it."

"Yep," Steve said, "right after that happened, I started to really live in my sex life, but outside it, too. I just felt a continuity between hard sex and making money and fixing the house and riding my motorcycle and . . . and . . . shit, and just everything."

"I think that's what's happening with me," Rick said.

They were silent for a moment, finishing their beer. Rick looked around the bar, watched a young man tied down to a table get his cock and balls shaved while somebody straddled him and fucked his face. Rick felt his prick start to get hard again, pressing against the damp denim.

Steve looked around the bar too, then looked back at Rick. He redeemed two more tokens, then leaned over and kissed Rick deeply for a moment.

"So, you said you'd had some slave training?" Steve asked. "What was that about?"

Rick swallowed his beer and said, "Well, you know, I go to the bars a lot and go home with leathermen, so over the years I've gotten a lot of training in bondage and torture. I love it, it's so fucking intense."

"Man, you're really different," Steve said. "You're brand new to multiple sex in public, but you've gone farther than most on your own. I like that."

"Yeah, that's it . . . it's the opening-up process that's letting me give myself to lots of men at once . . . it's almost spiritual, sacrificial, maybe communal, not like a private scene with one or two guys."

"You're fuckin' smart, man," Steve said, drinking more beer and looking around the bar again. "So, tell me a fantasy, something you'd like to do."

"What do you . . . you mean here?"

"Sure," Steve said, "give me a fantasy of something you'd like tonight, maybe we can set it up."

"Whoa, let me think . . ." Rick drank some more beer.

"C'mon, man, give me a fantasy. Tell Steve a bedtime story."

They both laughed and then Rick took another drink and started to confess some wishes.

"Well, for sure there's something I've always wanted, I've always wanted to get fucked by a whole bunch of men in a row, one after the other, ya know . . ." Rick faltered.

"Go on, man, I'm already getting hard."

Rick saw that Steve was rubbing his crotch. "You know, get tied up so that I'm not in control, so that I'm just a fucking hole for any guy to use, a place to stick his dick and shoot his cum."

"That's really hot, man," Steve said. "What's more, I think it can be done, here. Tonight. Right now."

"And sometimes I think about what it would be like to have a whole bunch of men watching me get used like this, maybe not even see some of the dudes who shove their cocks up my ass because somebody's sitting on my face or blindfolding me or something like that."

"Oh, yeah, that's great. I think it'll happen, man," Steve said, standing suddenly and walking over to a small group of men laughing and drinking beer in the corner. Rick sat and watched him, wondering why he had left so suddenly. He saw Steve talk for a long time with the hunky dudes, all of them the best examples of manhood, with big bulging arms, massive hairy chests, thick black moustaches, long uncut dicks curving down in front of them. Rick wondered how Steve knew them.

Rick saw Steve turn around and point to him, and then turn back to the group of men. They were looking at him now, very seriously, not laughing anymore. Steve turned and started to walk back to the bar, and then the group of men started to saunter over, following Steve and walking together straight towards Rick.

Steve got there first, and he put his hand out, touched Rick's thigh. The touch turned into a firm grip, then his other arm went around Rick's waist. Before he knew what was happening, he was being lifted off the barstool by the five huge studs, his pants were being torn off, thrown on the floor and a wet jock-strap was shoved into his mouth, gagging him. He struggled some, but still he trusted Steve for some reason, and besides there was not much he could do with five guys stripping him naked and carrying him through the bar like a little sex toy, some nude plaything.

The other men in the bar hooted and whistled, spraying beer on Rick's helpless body. Somebody reached out and tugged his dick and balls for a moment, someone else found a tit and pinched it, another two or three guys slapped his ass.

The men carried their prisoner to the slings, beneath the bright lights in the center of the largest room. They threw him into the leather and steel device, grabbing his wrists and ankles and strapping them in place in the sling. Rick wanted his body to be imprisoned by the masculine dudes. His prick was throbbing and slapping up against his belly. He wasn't scared at all; he was high, high on beer, but mostly high on the sudden sexual energy as he was possessed by the group of strange men and hauled off for their use.

He was in some sort of sexual ecstasy, and someone shoved a bottle of poppers under his nose, letting him breathe deeply of the sex incense, sending a wave of red-hot pleasure through his body. He felt like he was floating, his body resting completely in the sling, his arms and legs held in place by the leather restraints, the ten or twelve hot male hands holding his body, fondling his genitals, pinching his tits, squeezing and prodding his body like a rag doll.

Steve stood beside him, yanking the pissy jock out of Rick's mouth and bringing their lips together. "This is for you, man, a little fantasy life for you, baby," Steve whispered before plunging his tongue deep into Rick's mouth.

Rick felt fingers probing at his asshole, fondling and caressing his asscheeks, stroking his dick, tugging his nuts, fingers everywhere, hands on his chest, his stomach, his legs, smothering, burning hot male hands rubbing over his bound body. Rick felt globs of grease being slapped on his ass, warm, thick fingers probing his hot ass. Steve tongued his mouth, sucking on Rick's tongue and then fucking his mouth with his hot tongue.

Rick couldn't count how many fingers were inside his ass; he didn't care. He felt damn good, damn sexy, and he didn't care what anybody did, as long as it gave them pleasure, as long as he was the instrument of their pleasure. He felt the unmistakeable knob of a cockhead pressed against his greasy hole, then felt a huge mantool sliding into his ass, inching deeper and deeper, farther into the recesses of his bowels, slowly prying his rectum open wide. It was a big fucking dick, and Rick moaned in pleasure as the long weapon slid up into his belly.

Steve hoisted himself onto the frame of the sling, lowering his ass over Rick's face. Rick pushed his tongue out, begging for the brown manhole, dying to stick his wet tongue up that beautiful tight anus, up that ass that had probably taken many big dicks up inside.

Steve's ass found Rick's mouth, and Rick sucked on the hole, bathing it with hot spit, feeling the sphincter loosen up and open the hole to the invading tongue, letting the warm spit shoot up along the slick walls of the velvety shitchute.

Rick ate Steve's ass while some dude rammed his long thick manmeat in and out of his enslaved ass. The hands were still rubbing his body all over, pinching his tits, yanking painfully on his balls, squeezing and stroking his cock, but Rick's major sensations lay at the ramming cock in his ass and the hot sweaty asshole on his mouth.

The cock pounded up inside him, slamming the muscular belly of his assailant against the hard muscles of Rick's ass, each thrust impaling the slave on the monster organ. Rick was being made a slave to a raging hard-on, a soft wet place for a dick to find a way to squirt its cum, and still he shoved his tongue in and out of Steve's incredibly hot hole.

"Yeah, baby, eat that ass!" Steve ordered, "I'm watching a stud fuck your ass, man, you oughtta see it, man, you oughtta see the huge prick raping your butt!"

Rick could only moan as Steve spoke to him; then he heard the labored breathing of his fucker, heard him saying, "Take it, man, take this monster cock up your slimy hole. Yeah, baby, this thing is fucking the shit out of you, fucking worthless slave."

Other voices faded in and out: "Fuck him . . . yeah, man, fuck it . . . shove it up there . . . take it . . . c'mon, man, ram that motherfucker home . . . ram it all the way . . ."

Somebody spit on Rick's dick, again and again, and then he realized that it wasn't spit, it was someone jerking off onto his genitals, some man shooting cum onto his throbbing cock and balls. Then the pounding in his ass increased, growing more frantic, and Steve began to ride his ass up and down on Rick's tongue while the stud slammed his huge organ into Rick's slippery rectum.

"Take it, baby, here it comes . . ." Rick heard as he felt the violent pumping into his belly, felt the burning heat of hot cum squirt up inside him, felt the hunky dude grab his cum-covered cock and yank on it while he bucked his hips forward and shot his load deep into Rick's ass.

"Yeah, baby, that's an ass," the guy said, and then Rick heard him say to somebody else, "Yeah, you, go ahead."

And then there was another sudden thrust and a new cock was shoved up his ass. This one was longer and thinner, reaching deep inside Rick's velvet ass and probing his guts.

"Fuck him, man," Steve ordered, his loose ass covered with Rick's spit. "I want to see you shoot your load up that ass. Mix it with that other guy's load."

The long dick stuck his ass, probed it, slammed high and deep. Every thrust was an impalement, and Rick moved his hips in rhythm to meet the regular rapid poundings of the long manmeat.

Suddenly Steve raised himself from Rick's face, turned his body around as he held firm to the frame, then lowered his groin to Rick's face, smashing his heavy balls onto the slave's face, and then stuffing them into his mouth. "Lick 'em, man, suck my nuts," Steve ordered.

Rick sucked on the big balls, concentrating on the fat dick slapping against his forehead while the long prick was pumping his butt. The dick slid in and out faster and faster, and then, in a sudden hard thrust, the cock exploded a second load of burning liquid deep into his belly, pouring the male essence into his ass, flooding his rectum like an enema with molten white jism.

Steve pulled his ball sac out of Rick's mouth and thrust his huge pole into Rick's hot mouth until Rick swallowed the swollen head, sucked on the shaft and felt the wet slobbery balls resting up against his chin.

More dicks fucked his ass, two, three, four, maybe five . . . Rick couldn't keep count. They just kept slamming into his butt, dicks of every length, all of them huge, all of them rippling with throbbing veins, all of them ramming into his dripping asshole with such force that he knew he was being ripped apart. But the pleasure kept on coming, the cocks kept on thrusting, and Steve's sex weapon kept on sliding in and out of his throat.

Rick knew that he was just a hole, a big muscular wet butt-hole for Steve and his buddies to use, to tie up in the middle of the Caldron and rape, to use him as a worthless place to lay their slabs of dick, to massage their mansized pricks to orgasm. Harder and harder they fucked him, first a fat dick, then a long one, then a really huge monster that must have been twelve or thirteen inches long, opening him wide, prying his whole rectum wide apart for its pleasure, making room to shoot more cum. Hot love juice ran out of his ass, ran down the crack of his ass, spread and squirted around his balls and thighs, and one by one the big dicks filled him up, shot their heavy loads, and one by one they pulled out, satisfied, bloated, hanging heavy like horse dicks.

Rick felt a hot mouth close around his own shaft, and furiously he fucked that face, whoever it was, while Steve approached his own orgasm within the tight depths of Rick's open throat. Rick just sucked and licked while the long pole fucked his throat, ramming against his face as hard as the cocks had rammed against his ass. He felt Steve's nuts tighten, felt the dick grow very rigid, felt the uncontrollable thrusting and knew that a load was coming his way.

The hot mouth worked fast on Rick's engorged penis, sucking and sliding over the stiff prick, encircling it with incredible soft pleasure. Then Rick felt the moment approach when he knew it would be too late, when the cum would just burst through the huge throbbing dick and explode into the soft wet mouth. It was like a sixty-nine only different as he sucked on Steve's dick, felt the contractions start, felt the last few rams before the burning white liquid erupted in his mouth, pumping ounces and ounces of salty cum into his throat. Rick swallowed and sucked, tasting the sweet juice, feeling his own love juice come blasting up the length of his swollen tool, flowing up and up and then squirting, spurting like a wild fountain into the hot velvet mouth, emptying his cum like a stream of piss, shooting harder, bucking faster, slamming his dick all the way down the eager throat.

Rick milked all the cum from Steve's dick and the stud sucked the last of Rick's sweet jism. Steve climbed down and kissed Rick passionately, caressing his body and loosening the bonds at his wrists, and then at his ankles. Steve half collapsed on top of Rick, kissing him deeply, and they rested like that, gently caressing their necks and tits and lips.

Finally, Steve looked at Rick, saw the satisfaction there, smiled, and asked, "Got any more fantasies?"

PULSES AND PRESSURES

H E HAD ONE OF NEW YORK'S largest gay medical practices. He also had one of New York's largest cocks. And everybody knew it. The way he wore his white medical smock always open revealed the generous bulge in his tight jeans.

Half his patients feigned their illnesses as a means of getting past the lesbian receptionist and into the medical suites for their few precious minutes alone with Dr. James Calvin. His nurse, Jack, wasn't bad, either. As a matter of fact, Jack was a hunk, well known for his nocturnal wanderings in the city's leather district.

Together they were almost too much to bear—the hunky leather stud nurse and the handsome masculine doctor. Dr. Calvin was tall and blond, with a sharp blond moustache. Jack was tall and dark, with a thick black moustache. Both had sinister fantasies on their minds most of the time. And most of their patients shared the sleazy bent.

Richard hadn't lived in New York long before he realized it was time to get a checkup. He asked around, and the few gay men he knew all recommended him to Dr. Calvin's office. What a dude, what a hunk, you oughtta see his nurse! It was unanimous, so Rich called and made an appointment for the following Friday afternoon.

When Friday afternoon rolled around, Richard made his way to the doctor's office, in a fashionable building uptown. He was momentarily stunned as he entered the waiting area to see so many incredibly gorgeous hunks sitting around, flipping through old magazines, waiting to see Dr. Calvin.

He told the receptionist he was there, and then sat to wait. A handsome man in a dark suit smiled at Richard, then stood as his name was called. Richard looked up at the nurse, realizing that the studly hunk must be Jack. What a nurse! Richard felt his cock throb just at the sight of the hunky man, and to imagine the things he was reputed to do late at night by the waterfront.

At last it was Richard's turn to be admitted to the examining rooms. Richard willfully followed Jack to a small room near the back, watching the huge muscles of Jack's ass ripple beneath the tight jeans. Jack wore a smart white jacket, the only allusion to medicine in his total masculine garb—jeans, black leather boots, a studded leather belt.

"Okay," Jack said, "What's the trouble?"

"Nothing," Rich answered. "Nothing at all. I just wanted to get a standard STD checkup."

"Great," Jack said, and then added, "been out and around a lot lately, eh?"

"Well, sort of . . ." Rich admitted, thinking of the scores of studs he had serviced at the pier, at the Mine Shaft, in the park.

"We'll get you fixed just fine," Jack said, arranging various medical items, and then proceeding to take the samples necessary. "You're a new patient, aren't you?" Jack asked.

"Yes, that's right . . ." Rich answered.

Just then the door flew open, and the most macho man Rich had ever seen swept into the room, emanating charisma and sex and horniness and masculinity. The doctor was hunky, blond, his bright blue eyes twinkling mischievously.

The beautiful doctor glanced at Rich's chart, winked at Jack, then told Rich to strip. "Might as well give you a complete going-over while you're here," the doctor said, watching appreciatively as Rich quickly stripped off his shirt, jeans, and tight briefs.

Jack stared openly at Rich's generous sexual equipment.

"Good," was all the doctor said, moving around behind Rich and holding his stethoscope up to his back.

"Breathe deeply," the doctor suggested, pressing the cold metal disc against Rich's taut muscled back. He listened for a moment, then let his bulging crotch press lightly against Rich's nude ass.

Rich noticed the gentle bump, and his prick began to fatten. The scene was too horny for him: a hot leather stud as a nurse, and a gorgeous hunky blond with a huge dick as a doctor, both holding that mysterious medical power over him.

Jack saw the fattening dick and whistled. "Look here, doctor, this one needs some real medical aid!"

Rich blushed, but just then the doctor locked the door to the examining room and ordered Rich to bend over the examining table, "for a routine anal exam . . ."

Rich was growing more excited as the medical exam turned into a bondage scene. Jack quickly unbuttoned his jeans and let his giant cock and balls hang free, and the doctor greased up his anuscope and began to slide it into Rich's tight asshole.

"Just relax," the doctor said, lightly slapping each ass cheek with the palm of his hand. The steel probe slid easily into the greased hole, and then the doctor bent to look up inside the rectum.

"All right," he said, "that looks damn good up there, all pink and shiny and inviting . . ."

Just then there was a brief pause, a moment of tension as the doctor continued to look inside Rich, and as Jack stood near Rich's face, his cock and balls hanging free. But the moment passed when Rich began to move his hips around, trying to enjoy the probing medical instrument.

Jack saw the hip motion and knew that yes, it was all right to proceed.

Quickly he grabbed a long strip of strong cotton gauze and wrapped it tightly around Rich's wrists, pulling his hands behind his back tightly. In this way, Rich was bent over the examining table, his ass stuck up in the air with a steel anuscope thrust inside it, his torso laid out flat, facedown the length of the table. The table was just short enough that Rich's face rested right on the end of the table.

Jack moved his dick in front of Rich's face. "Suck on that thing, baby," he ordered, gently slapping the fat member across Richard's face, lips, his flickering tongue. Then, suddenly, Jack shoved the length of his stiff pole into the open mouth, forcing it deep into the captive throat.

Rich began to suck hard, opening his throat to the invading tool. He was unsure what the doctor was doing, but the anuscope was still in place, keeping his upturned asshole pried open. He heard the sound of the doctor preparing something, and then he felt the sudden prick of a needle in his arm.

Rich tensed for a moment but then the doctor said, "Relax, Rich, just a bit of injected Valium to make you really enjoy the scene." And sure enough, within a matter of seconds, Rich noticed his head start to swim, a sudden dizzy sensation giving way to an incredible docility. Rich was really calm now, and his throat opened easily as Jack continued to plunge the full length of his long manmeat in and out of Richard's slurping throat.

"Good boy," the doctor said, slowly easing out the anuscope. "Think you can handle the biggest dick in New York?"

Rich barely nodded his head before he felt a huge thing pressing at his butt, something that felt like a baseball bat. But the Valium was working well, and like a rubber band his sphincter stretched wide open, quickly admitting the thickest piece of manly sex-meat Rich had ever felt. With two huge dicks stuck inside his drug-relaxed body, Rich felt like he was floating, suspended at either end by hard cocks.

"Yeah, a healthy ass indeed," the doctor moaned as he thrust his hips forward hard, slamming the huge tool up Richard's hot ass. "Take it, patient, it's the biggest fucking horse dick in Manhattan."

But then Jack pulled his cock out of Richard's mouth and stepped back. He watched as the doctor's giant dick worked on the upturned ass. "I think we need a little urinalysis on this patient, doctor, whatta ya think?"

"Sure, go ahead," the doctor said, laughing at some secret

joke as he continued to pound away. Rich simply moaned and writhed in pleasure at the abuse; he was in heaven with the huge prick up his ass, the Valium in his blood.

Jack brought a small bottle over, the kind used for collecting urine specimens. But instead of offering it to Rich, he stood directly in front of Richard's face and began to shoot his own hot piss into the glass. Rich watched in fascination as the clear stream shot into the glass, and when the liquid threatened to overflow the top, he wondered if Jack could stop pissing.

Jack slapped his face and yelled. "Drink that flowing piss, man," and began to pour the steady stream of piss into Richard's mouth. Richard drank the piss greedily, feeling the hot stream land on his tongue, then run in little rivulets out the corner of his mouth. He took big gulps of the urine, swallowing and swallowing as Jack poured more of the stuff into the bound patient.

"Looks hot," the doctor said, slowing up on his poundings, and then yanking his huge hard-on free of the sloppy greasy ass. "Make him drink that piss in the specimen jar."

"Yeah, baby, swallow that stuff," Jack ordered, holding the filled specimen glass to Richard's lips and forcing him to drink piss from the glass. "Ooohh, that's good," the doctor said, walking around in front.

It was the first view Rich had got of the big dick that had just been fucking his ass. Rich couldn't believe that anything could be that big. It *was* as big as a baseball bat, all thick and bloated, hanging heavy and curved like a horse dick. The thing was monstrous and uncircumcised, the foreskin pulled part way back, the whole huge tool glistening with KY jelly.

When Rich had swallowed the last drop of piss, the doctor stepped up and said he'd better check out Rich's tonsils. With that he slid the long greasy pole into Rich's salty-tasting piss-filled mouth, slowly easing the monster dick into the throat, forcing it past the relaxed gag response, gently beginning to pump the organ in and out.

All Rich could do was moan as the weapon forced its way down his throat. It wasn't long before Jack was behind Rich, aiming his hard prick towards the loose shit-hole, pressing the engorged head against the opening and shoving his dick inside.

"Oh, man, this is a damn hot ass," Jack said, as he sunk the whole length of his dick into the rectum. He slammed his prick as hard as he could, enjoying the sensation of the hot slick flesh clinging round his pumping cock.

"Take that dick, man, let me see you suck the doctor's dick," the doctor said, slapping Rich on the face and ramming his dick in and out. "Suck it . . ."

Both the doctor and the nurse rammed their mantools into Rich, using his body like some toy, some piece of soft flesh designed to satisfy their pricks. They pumped and worked, groaning and slapping Rich, coming closer and closer to shooting their loads.

"We have patients waiting," Jack said, slamming his dick again and again into the upturned ass.

"Yeah . . ." the doctor agreed, sliding his tool again into the hot wet mouth.

"Oh, I'm gonna shoot . . ." Jack cried out, ramming himself as hard and fast as he could into Rich.

"Yeah, me too . . ." the doctor said.

And then, all at once, Rich felt like he might split in two as the monstrous dicks swelled up even larger, growing fat and stiff, pulsing wild with cum coursing up and up and out, exploding in hot white rivers of burning jism in Rich's ass and mouth.

"Grrr . . . take the cum . . ." they cried out as they shot their heavy loads, flooding his ass and throat with love juice. "Drink it . . ."

The two finished their fucking and pulled their dicks out of the patient. Jack rolled Rich over and noticed that he was covered with sweat, but his face was pure bliss.

"Oh, yeah, doc," Rich whispered, glancing around at the two of them, a satisfied grin fastened to his drugged-out face. "Fuck me more, again, I think I'll need a medical exam every week . . ."

His voice trailed off and Jack smiled. "I'd like to see you jerk him off," the doctor said to Jack. "Let's see if his prostate works okay."

"Good idea," Jack agreed, reaching for Rick's own stiff pole and beginning to stroke it. Jack ran his hand up and down the length of the shaft, trailing his fingers in circles around the glistening head. The big thing throbbed after being neglected so long, and Jack fingered the shiny pre-cum fluid, rubbing the slippery juice all around the dickhead. Rich moaned and ground his hips around, feeling the cum begin to boil in his loins.

"He looks good like that," the doctor said, appreciating the way Rich lay on his back, his arms tied together underneath him, his huge hard-on sticking up in the air, getting stroked by Jack's fast-working hand.

"I'm gonna shoot!" Rich said, thrusting his hips forward as the hand kept on sliding up and down on his slippery dick. "Oh, fucking yeah . . ."

It was evident that Rich was about to shoot, and the doctor grabbed the specimen glass that had held Jack's piss, handing it to Jack.

Just then Rich's huge prick exploded in a wild spray of cum, pumping ounces and ounces of the hot liquid into the specimen jar that Jack held over the cockhead.

When Rich was finished filling the glass with his cum, Jack held it up to the light, examined it for a moment, and then brought it back to Rich. The doctor helped Rich sit upright, and then Jack put the jar to Richard's lips, ordered him to drink his own cum.

"Drink it, man, swallow your cum," Jack said, tipping the jar back and pouring the fluid into Rich's mouth. "We believe in recycling!" The doctor and Jack both laughed at this humiliation as they watched Rich finish the last of his own cum from the jar.

Jack untied Rich and helped him to dress. The Valium had worn off just a bit, but for the most part Rich still felt damn high, damn good, damn relaxed.

"I think you're pretty healthy," the doctor said as he stuffed that giant dick back into his pants and put the stethoscope back around his neck.

"Yes," Jack agreed, "but I think he better come back next week for a follow up. How 'bout it?"

"No problem," Rich said, smiling. He was still glowing. "No problem at all. I have medical insurance."

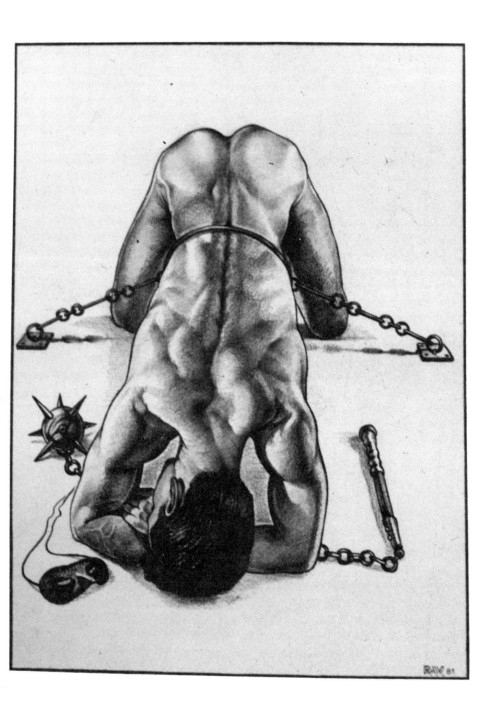

SIR KRUGER

T HUNDER ROLLED OVER SAN FRANCISCO the night the tropical storm moved in. Young Paul Richards sat up in bed, listening to the storm and reading a popular gay newspaper. He was hornier than hell, all pumped up from too much energy, not enough sex, definitely not enough of the hard-core abusive sex he loved and craved so much.

He turned to the pink section of the paper, the pull-out part that was packed with classified ads, ads for everything from real estate to transexual prostitutes into SCAT and filth.

Well, Paul thought, I'll pass on the transexuals. He scanned the ads, one by one, first the personals, and then the ads for "Models, Masseurs." He was getting hornier with each ad. Some of the personals sounded really hot, but he was frustrated by no phone numbers, just a box number to be written to with a pic, then the wait for the reply. He wanted some heavy action, and he wanted it now, tonight.

Thunder cracked as he read down the columns of men for hire. Really hot studs, hung, cut and uncut, muscular, tops, bottoms, leather, western, Levis, chains . . . it was all there for the taking, all for a few dollars.

For years Paul had studied the classified ads in this paper, and for years he had wanted to do what he was thinking about doing tonight. He'd always stopped short of picking up the phone and dialing, though. It wasn't the money he minded; he had plenty of that from working his ass off all week. It's just that he usually went out to his favorite clubs, like THE SLOT, or the CALDRON. He'd find okay heavy sex there, but he knew that he wanted more than most of the guys were going to give him in the clubs.

His dick was hard as he continued to read the ads. He pulled on the head, drawing his thick foreskin back and exposing the glistening sensitive head of his long cock. Fuck, I'm horny! he thought, taking his hand away and reading the last few ads.

Suddenly his dick grew really fat and started to throb. He'd found the ad he was hoping for, the perfect description of everything he had always wanted:

SIR KRUGER

Huge uncut thick horsemeat German leathermaster will abuse obedient slaves in his well-equipped medieval dungeon. Slaves must submit to my demands: you will be stripped, laid out, chained, shaved, whipped, tortured, tits worked, balls beaten, pissed on, fucked, spit on, humiliated, and thrown out. Cum to your demanding Master and be prepared to serve. No limitations respected, no fantasies fulfilled. You will service my enormous uncut meat as I order you to. Call now.

There was a phone number given at the end of the ad. Paul looked down at his own big uncut prick, now pounding up along his belly and dripping heavy drops of shiny pre-cum. He knew he wanted to do it. He knew he had to do it. He picked up the phone and dialed.

The phone rang five times, six, seven . . . Paul decided to hang up just as the other end of the line was engaged.

"Yes?" a deep, thick voice asked.

"Is Sir Kruger there?" Paul asked.

"This is Sir Kruger."

There was silence, and Paul realized that he would have to solicit the transaction.

"I, uh . . . I was reading the ads in the pink classifieds, and, uh, your ad sounded really like, maybe, well, it really intrigued me." Paul felt tense, but very excited.

"Yes, okay," the deep voice said.

Paul gained a little more confidence as the excitement pulled him into the inevitable encounter. "Well, I was wondering how much your, uh, fee was, and if maybe you had any openings tonight?"

"Certainly. I am available at once, if that is convenient for you. My modeling fee is $75.00, and I place no time limit."

"No limit?" Paul was incredulous.

"That's correct. I prefer to take my time with my subjects, in order that I might most adequately and fully make use of them before I permit their passage out."

Paul was fucking horny by now. The slow, courteous speech puzzled him. The man seemed too much of a gentleman, but then, there was an icy edge to his tone, a sense of strength, or power.

"Okay, that's okay," Paul said. "I can come over right now, too."

"I will expect you within half an hour," Sir Kruger said. He gave Paul the address—deep in the heart of the South of Market area. The last thing he told Paul was to wear a jockstrap, drink some beer, and "Do not be late. I wait for no one." With that, he hung up.

Paul jumped out of bed, dashed under the shower, and toweled himself dry. His big uncircumcised cock hung heavy over his giant nuts, curving down over the big ball sac like a horse's dick. He put on the jockstrap, then jeans, a black t-shirt, black engineer boots, and, as a last thought, he reached up and took his slave collar off the wall and fastened it around his neck. He grabbed a couple of beers and left to drive down to Folsom Street. He had about fifteen minutes to get across town, without being late.

He just made it, pulling up at the old Victorian on one of those little alleys that winds its way across the Folsom. The place was dark and forboding. There was no light anywhere, and the place seemed especially dark because it was painted a dull grey. Paul checked the address again, downed the last of his second beer, adjusted his collar, and climbed the dozen stone steps to a heavy wooden door. There was an iron knocker, and Paul reached up and pounded it three times.

After a long silence, Paul heard heavy footsteps approaching the door. It opened wide, revealing a long dark hallway illuminated only by two black candles set along the wall. It was almost spooky, but somehow very sexual. The storm kept up, and just as Paul turned his attention to the man standing in the hall, a flash of lightning suddenly illuminated the tall, leather-clad Master.

Paul's eyes widened at this vision of overwhelming maleness. The man was tall, about 6'3", extremely handsome with a very Saturnine beard. He wore black motorcycle chaps, a studded leather jock, and his muscular torso was covered with a steel and leather body harness, criss-crossing his chest, over his shoulders, and circling his waist.

Paul was extremely turned-on by the leather stud. His big dick bulged against his jockstrap, pushing the crotch of his jeans into a big fat bulge. He knew that even though he was scared, he was going to like serving the studmaster.

"Come in," Sir Kruger beckoned.

Paul walked into the hall and shook the man's extended hand. "Hi," was all that Paul could think to say. He could smell the leather, the sweat, a heady aroma that aroused his animal instincts to fuck.

"My fee?" the man said.

"Oh, yeah," Paul said, reaching into his pocket and handing over a fifty, twenty, and a ten. He hadn't had the right change, so he said, "The extra is because I didn't have a five, and I figured the extra five might pay for just that extra meanness I need." As soon as the words were out of his mouth, Paul realized that he had said too much.

The leathermaster fixed a cold stare at him and said only, "Very well."

There was a moment of silence, and then Sir Kruger said, "Strip. Right now. Right here. Put your clothes on the floor." He picked up a watch and said, "You have exactly thirty seconds to strip yourself completely naked, so you better get to it." He kept on looking at the watch as Paul began frantically to strip off his shirt, jeans, boots, and jockstrap.

Sir Kruger kept talking: "Each second beyond thirty seconds that you take to remove your clothes represents a slash of the whip, to be delivered in good measure."

This frightened Paul into fumbling with his shoes. Fuck, he thought to himself as he tangled his pants and socks and boots in a big mess.

"Ten seconds left," the leathermaster said.

Paul stepped out of one pant leg and boot, and reached down to untangle the other leg.

"Thirty seconds!" Sir Kruger snapped. "Now you suffer . . . five, six, seven, eight, nine, ten . . ."

Paul stepped free and stood naked before the man.

"Very good, slave," he spit into Paul's face. "Only thirteen seconds over." He put the watch down. "Thirteen slashes with the whip is capable of providing a great deal of stimulation if applied to the genitals."

Paul shuddered at the thought, but his long cock stood straight out from his body, oozing pre-cum and throbbing already. Sir Kruger looked down at it and said, "That's nice meat, but it is a bit too anxious. Perhaps it needs to be tamed."

The studmaster walked over to one of the black candles on the wall, picked it up, and carried it back to where Paul stood, his engorged prick still jutting out from his well-muscled body.

"Do not move," the man ordered. "Do not wince. Do not utter a sound."

With that he turned the candle sideways, letting the hot molten wax drip onto the shiny bulbous head of Paul's gigantic hard-on. He couldn't help but cry out, which earned him a rough slap on the face. The hot wax was setting up firm on his dick-head and the Master poured more wax down the length of the stiff rod, covering it with hardening wax.

It hurt at first, but within a couple of seconds Paul began to enjoy the burning sensation. It did not reduce his erection, though, and Sir Kruger had known that it wouldn't.

He held the candle upright and said, "That did not work.

But I know a method that will work." He reached between Paul's legs, grabbed his big nut sac, squeezed as hard as he could, and tugged the big balls forward. With the candle he tipped wax all over the balls, all the while grabbing them like a vise. Pain shot through Paul's body, and his dick softened at once.

"That's much better," the Master said. "Stand for inspection," he ordered, returning the candle to its holder in the wall. He circled round the naked young man before him, looking him over like a bidder at an auction. He noted that the ass was round, firm, and tight, the chest hunky, smooth, defined, the face very attractive, and the dick enormous.

"Let's test the waters," the Master said, hauling back and slapping Paul's tender ass. The cheek grew red as the master slapped it a second time. Then he ran his hand down the crack between the cheeks, finding the soft puckered asshole. He fingered it for a moment, feeling the tight hole pucker up at the touch of the teasing finger.

He pulled his finger away and shoved it into Paul's mouth. "Lick that finger, slave," he ordered, "get it wet; it's the only lube you're getting."

Paul slurped on the finger, coating it with his hot saliva. Sir Kruger pulled his finger out of Paul's mouth, brought his hand back down over the firm round buns, found the little hole and shoved his finger all the way in. Paul gasped at the sensation, not really pain, but he managed to remain quiet as the thick finger twisted, pried, and fucked his asshole.

"That will serve my needs very well," the Master said, pulling his finger out of the asshole. He knew that Paul was clean, and this pleased him. Nevertheless, he shoved the finger back into Paul's mouth and ordered him to lick it clean. Paul sucked on the finger that had just probed his ass, licking it clean of any sweat and ass juice.

The thunder cracked again, lightning briefly lighting the hall, then bathing it in darkness again. Rain beat down on the roof, and Sir Kruger barked out a sudden order.

"Down on the floor, you piece of shit. Sit on your ass and

spread those legs wide."

Paul dropped to the floor at once, feeling the cold wood on his ass. He spread his legs apart, noting that his big ball sac nestled on the floor, his dickhead curved down to the wooden slats.

"Look down at your cock and balls, slave," he ordered. Paul looked down. Sir Kruger slowly walked forward, his heavy leather boots crunching the floor. He stepped between Paul's legs, and with both feet forced Paul's legs further apart.

Now Paul's dick and nuts were really vulnerable. "Put those hands behind your back," the Master ordered. "Watch me step on your useless privates." He placed the toe of his boot on the head of Paul's dick and ground it into the floor. Paul let out a low moan as the cleats of the boot pressed painfully into the sensitive uncut head.

The Master lifted his boot, pushed the cock to one side, and slowly pressed his boot down on the big balls. He let up for a moment, pushed the balls around on the floor so that they were perfectly centered between the spread legs, and then brought his foot down in one sudden crunch. Paul howled in pain-pleasure, his dick springing up into instant erection.

"Ah," the Master said, "genitorture pleases you. We will see to that soon enough." He let up the boot and stood back. "On your hands and knees," he ordered sharply. Paul got on all fours and waited.

The Master walked to a wooden bureau in the corner, opened a drawer, and produced a steel leash. He walked back to the waiting slave and attached the leash to the collar. "You are my dog," he said, "follow me."

With that he walked forward, tugging on the leash and forcing Paul to crawl along behind the leatherman on his hands and knees. Sir Kruger led him to a side door at the end of the hall. He opened it and began to descend steep wooden stairs. Paul had to struggle to manage the stairs on all fours, but somehow he found himself at the bottom, on a cold cement floor.

It was pitch black—wherever he was—and the sounds of the raging storm were muted, very distant now as the Master pulled on the leash and led Paul forward in the blackness. Paul lost all sense of direction, but just as he was about to panic, he saw a thin slice of red light at the end of what appeared to be a narrow stone-enshrouded tunnel. The Master bent down and continued through the tunnel. Paul crawled along behind.

They emerged into a medieval dungeon of stone. Paul was amazed that anything of the kind even existed in San Francisco, but here he was, somewhere in the bowels of the Folsom district, in a chamber beneath the house.

Paul glanced around him in the dim red glow. Chains and manacles seemed to hang from everywhere. Along the walls were assorted instruments of torture—whips, branding irons, weights, chains, dildoes of every size and shape, leather devices, hoods. Though he realized that none of these were more than he could handle, the cumulative effect of the sudden visual image was overwhelming. Paul's dick stiffened.

"Alright, dog," Sir Kruger said, dropping the leash and turning to face the young man on the floor. "This is my workroom. This is your prison. This is where you offer yourself completely to me. This is where you suffer great pleasure."

Paul was silent, looking up at the Master standing over him, his leather-clad legs spread wide apart, his hairy muscular chest beginning to glisten a thin film of sweat. Somehow, the room was very warm, despite the cold grey stones.

There was a long dull moment. Paul waited; Sir Kruger stood motionless. Paul looked up at him; Sir Kruger simply stared. Silence settled in the dungeon, and Paul began to wonder what would happen. The Master continued to stare, fixing a cold, sinister gaze at his slave. Paul debated in his mind—should he say something? Make a request? Get up and leave? Wait? He was sorting his feelings, testing his fears, his desires, weighing the long moment. Then he knew he wanted it.

Sir Kruger watched the slave wait, saw the fear and worry in his eyes, noticed the softening dick. He was patient; it was a crucial moment. Although the young man had bought this scene, Sir Kruger watched closely for the interior struggle to resolve. What finally registered in Paul's face was the sign that convinced the Master that Paul was indeed ready to give himself over for a workout.

Without breaking the stare, Sir Kruger breathed deeply, noticed the flicker of eagerness in the slave's eyes, and suddenly demanded:"Kneel!"

Paul pulled himself upright, bringing himself to a kneeling position before Sir Kruger. Instinctively he placed his hands behind his back, a gesture that Sir Kruger interpreted as a good sign of a fairly well-trained slave; he would have his way.

It was time to get down to business. Sir Kruger took a pair of handcuffs, fastened them around Pauls's wrists behind his back. Then he took a thin leather strap and secured the handcuffs tight against Paul's body by wrapping the strap tight around the slave's waist. Next he took a length of chain, fastened it at one end to the handcuffs, ran the other end up through the D-ring in the slave collar, pulled it tight, and secured it with a small padlock.

Paul was tense but excited as his Master enslaved him in bondage. Next thing he knew, a leather hood was being placed over his head. There was a hole for his mouth, two small nostril slits, and two narrow slits for vision. The leather hood muffled the sounds of Sir Kruger as he moved across the room, and the narrow eye slits restricted his vision to whatever was immediately in front of his face. Paul felt himself relaxing. Somehow the hood was making him another person; he had strangely become someone who was faceless and thus without inhibition. He would do anything.

The Master returned and stood before him, holding a tall can of beer. "Like a beer, kid?" he asked. Paul nodded his head. "Then here, have a drink." Sir Kruger held the can at Paul's mouth, tipped it, and let him drink. For just a moment Paul flashed on Communion, on sipping the wine at the Cathedral, but then he tasted the bittersweet taste of piss. The Master was feeding him recycled beer!

"Yes, slave, that beer is recycled. It is the only beer you deserve in your place of humiliation. Drink it!"

Paul hesitated for a moment, but a sudden slap across the face changed his mind and he obeyed. After all, he liked to drink piss. He couldn't remember how many times he had knelt to take the hot piss of hunky studs at the CALDRON.

He drank eagerly now, tasting the stale beer, wishing that he were drinking from the source. The Master knew this would be the case, and he quickly dropped the beer can, aimed his huge dick at the slave's mouth, and let loose with a stream of burning piss. Paul moaned and greedily drank it down, taking the long prick in his mouth and feeling the strong river of yellow liquid flood over his tongue, drop out the corners of his mouth, and fill him up as he swallowed it.

Paul wished that he could see the big dick that was flooding his mouth with hot urine, but the eye slits in the hood weren't big enough. But he could judge that the prick was a hefty chunk of meat, very thick, very heavy, and Paul flicked his tongue out just long enough to discover that yes, Sir Kruger was uncut.

"That is a very good slave," he said as Paul milked the last drops from the heavy cock. "You like piss, that is good. I want you to piss in this cup, now," he ordered. Paul felt a cup held beneath his throbbing dick. He tried to concentrate on anything to soften his dick so that he could piss. Finally, he managed to let go with a strong stream of his own piss, filling the cup completely and then overflowing onto the floor. When the piss stopped, Sir Kruger placed the cup on the floor, undid the bonds at Paul's wrists, and ordered him to lie on the floor on his back.

"Lay back in the puddle of piss, slave; that's my piss and your piss. Lay down in it!"

"Yes, Sir," Paul answered as he lay out flat in the puddle of warm piss. It completely soaked his back, the back of his legs, his ass. His big balls hung down to the floor, and he could feel the wetness there, too.

"Put your arms out and spread your legs," Sir Kruger commanded. Paul did, and the Master attached wrist and ankle restraints to his slave, then chained these to four steel rings embedded in the floor. Paul was now chained down, spread-eagle in a pool of piss.

The Master knelt down beside Paul and pulled the hood off. Roughly he kissed him, forcing his tongue deep into the slave's hot, salty mouth. He could taste his piss there, and as he kissed Paul violently, he ran his strong hands over the body stretched out before him.

Paul responded heavily, his fat prick throbbing up against his belly, oozing pre-cum over his navel. He wanted desperately to wrap his arms around this beautiful strong man, but he was held firmly in place by the restraints.

The Master continued to kiss him, running his hand down between Paul's legs and fondling his big bull balls. He wrapped his fist around the nuts, and as he gently teased his tongue across Paul's lips, he tightened his grip, grabbing the vulnerable nuts like a vise, tighter and tighter, wrenching and tugging.

Paul arched his body in absolute pleasurepain, straining against his bonds, torn between submission and desire, between being a sex toy and wanting to passionately make love to this handsome stud.

Sir Kruger's other hand found Paul's tender pink tits. He fondled one and then the other, following this with terrific pinches and tugging.

"Yeah, slave, feel that hand yanking your balls? I could fucking pull them off if I wanted to, eh?"

"Yes, Sir," Paul said.

"Feel me work that tit? You like that? Like feeling that titwork, that ball stretchin'? I'm gonna torture your tits and balls, gonna tie you up by your balls and fuck the holy shit out of you, gonna make you beg for mercy and then gag you with a filthy piss-soaked jockstrap."

"Please, sir," Paul whispered. "Please use me." He gasped as Sir Kruger let go of his balls, raised his hand in the air, and then brought it down across the cock and balls.

"OOUUH," Paul yelped when the hand slapped his dick and nuts. "Please, Sir . . ."

There was another slap, and another, and Paul was flooded with conflicting sensations of utter pain and indescribable pleasure. Never before had he endured such torture, but his dick remained powerfully rigid, reacting to the repeated beating of his genitals.

"Okay, enough," Sir Kruger said, sitting back on his honches. "That hair is coming off now." He got up and got a razor and a bar of shaving soap. He dipped the shaving brush into the cup full of piss, soaking the brush completely, and then he lathered it up with the soap and began to work the suds over Paul's groin. When it was glistening wet and soapy, Sir Kruger took the razor and slowly, methodically shaved the hair from Paul's groin, cock and balls.

Paul lay and watched as the shiny steel blade passed over his cock, slid over his big globes, watched as each stroke of the blade revealed smooth pink sensitive skin. When the job was done, Paul saw that his huge prick looked even bigger jutting up directly from his groin, undisguised by any dark hair. Sir Kruger fondled the nuts and dick, feeling the smoothness. His hands passed over the shaved area, toying with Paul's genitals as though they were nothing but toys in a department store.

"Okay, slave, let's see how well you can follow orders and provide a little show." Sir Kruger unfastened Paul's wrists and ankles. "Stay there!" he ordered, reaching over and picking up a leather ball stretcher.

Paul watched as the Master wrapped the ball stretcher around his nuts, fastening it tight and adjusting it so that his nuts were pulled low in the big sac. There was a short chain attached to the ball stretcher, and on the end of the chain was a clasp.

"Up on your hands and knees," Sir Kruger barked. "Stick that ass up in the air."

Paul got on all fours and tilted his firm ass upwards. Sir Kruger grabbed the chain and attached a heavy five-pound weight to the clasp. Suddenly he let it fall to the floor, but is was enough to yank hard on Paul's nuts, sending a shooting pain coursing through his groin.

"We're gonna have you drag some weight around, boy," the Master said, attaching another five pound chunk of lead to the slave's balls. Now Paul had ten pounds of lead attached to his balls.

"Crawl around the room, slave!" the Master ordered, standing up and kicking Paul's ass forward with his boot. "C'mon, get moving!" he ordered, reaching down and slapping the ass hard.

Paul began to crawl around the outer perimeter of the chamber, pulling the lead behind him. The Master laughed and called him a donkey. Paul continued to crawl around the room, dragging the heavy weight along the floor by his nuts. The metal scraped against the stone floor, and occasionally the weights would hang up on a crack in the floor, and Paul would endure agony as he pressed forward, pulling the heavy lead between his legs.

When he had gone all around the room, Sir Kruger took the chain off the ball stretcher and patted Paul on the head, like a pet dog. "Very good, shithead," he commended, and then he spit in Paul's face once, twice, and then a third time.

"I spit on you, fucker, understand me? You're here to serve my cock, right?"

"Yes, Sir," Paul answered, breathing heavily from the work of dragging all the weight around the room.

"And I think it's about time for you to start." Sir Kruger went over and pulled a low table into the middle of the room. It was covered with padded black leather. "Tell me what you want, slave," he said, adjusting the table and piling up different things around it.

"I want to serve you," Paul answered simply.

"How?"

"In any way you want..."

"In what ways do you like?"

Paul wondered if he were being baited, but said, "As you wish, Sir, please use your dick on me, shove it down my throat, shove it up my ass, fuck me, spit on me, piss on me, just use me... Sir... uh, whatever, Sir..."

"Very well," he said, suddenly grabbing Paul by the waist and hauling him over to the leather-topped table. He put him down on the table on his stomach. It was a short table, and when Sir Kruger adjusted Paul on top of it, his chin just rested on one end, his hips on the other. His legs hung free, and quickly the Master took his ankles and tied them down to the legs of the table. Then he tied Paul's hands to the front legs of the table, and stood back to survey his handiwork.

Paul lay face down, his head supported by the end of the table. His arms and legs were tied down, so that it appeared as though Paul was hugging the table. His ass hung off the other end, his cock and balls dangling in the air.

The Master nodded his approval at the site, took a long leather rope, looped it through the D-ring in the ball stretcher, tied it tight and tied the other end of the leather rope to a hook under the table. This held Paul's hips and ass firmly in place. He could not raise his hips without yanking painfully on his taut nuts.

"Very fine, Slave," the Master said, walking around in front of Paul, dangling his heavy uncut manmeat in the upturned face.

For the first time Paul got a good look at the huge organ. The thing was long and fat, uncut, and throbbing blue veins ran the length of the monster, giving it a rough, animalistic texture.

"You're gonna feel this thing in your ass and in your throat, asshole," he said, stroking the huge piece into a raging hard-on. "You want to feel this thing invade your holes? Want to feel it open you up and pump you full of hot white cum?"

"Yes, Sir . . . please, Sir . . . oh . . . yes . . ."

The Master pulled back the tight foreskin and forced the cheesy horse dick into Paul's velvet hot mouth. "HMMMM . . ." Paul moaned as he sucked on the invading pole. Sir Kruger pushed his hips forward, burying his groin into Paul's face, forcing the long tool deep down his throat. Paul swallowed eagerly as the big dick pried him open.

"Yeah, baby, suck that monster, suck it . . ."

Paul gagged for a moment and then began to slurp on the piece of meat like it was candy, sucking and licking and rolling his tongue as the dick raped his face back and forth. "Yeah, slave-hole, take it . . ."

Sir Kruger pumped his cock into Paul's face a few more

times, enjoying the hot wet mouth on his hard-on before withdrawing it and coating it with warm, greasy lube. Paul watched as the thick hand slipped grease onto the long mantool, knowing full well that this huge meat was going to pry his ass open.

The Master walked around behind Paul and rubbed some grease over the hole. He took his greasy hand away from the shiny little buns and let go with a hard slap. Paul gasped when he felt the stinging slap, but he could not move his hips or his arms or legs. He could only wait for the next hit, which came with equal force on his other ass-cheek.

"I'm going to slap this thing raw," the Master said, continuing to whack the hell out of the tight pink ass. Paul closed his eyes in painful ecstasy, enjoying the heavy beating. His ass felt red-hot, burning, ready for a big fat man-sized dick to be shoved up inside it all the fucking way.

As quickly as the beating had begun, it stopped. Next Paul felt a huge dickhead pressing against his tight puckered asshole. The heat of the blood-engorged organ was incredible. Paul felt the round knob of the raping dick force its way into his hole, pressing beyond the sphincter and prying its way deep into the velvety red softness of his waiting shit-chute.

The greasy slab of dick slid up inside him, pushing the burning walls of his aching rectum open, parting the wet flesh inch by inch as the Master sunk more of his enormous tool in Paul's ass. With one final short thrust, the whole chunk of meat was buried in Paul's ass, throbbing and pulsing in the clinging tube of slimy warm flesh. He slowly began to stroke, relishing squeezing the base of his fat cock while the big head began to rub the slippery depths of a hot ass.

"Oh, yeah, slave baby, you're getting fucked by your Master..."

"Please, Sir, fuck me, ... please..."

"Getting fucked by your Master, getting raped by a fucking stud."

With that he began to pound in earnest, ramming his dick into the waiting hole, impaling Paul's bound form on his swollen horse-meat. He placed his hands on Paul's lower back, near each hip, and pressed down firmly as he plowed the tight buns, pumping his tool in and out of the satin-soft flesh. The slick walls clung to his thrusting sword, massaging the wet chute, pushing up against Paul's swollen prostate.

Paul's stiff dick had slipped in between his belly and the leather table. Every time Sir Kruger forced his dick into Paul's hole, the powerful thrust would force his own cock to rub against the leather, wet now from the generous oozing of pre-cum.

The Master kept pounding his belly against the chained boy's ass. He slapped the ass-cheeks hard with his hand, ramming his engorged penis deep into the ass.

"Take it, slave, fucking take it," the Master yelled as he plowed Paul's asshole.

"Yeah, slave, feel your man's hard-on rape your worthless ass." He spit on Paul's back, rammed his dick in hard, then pulled it out.

Paul felt empty with the huge piece of meat missing from his shit-chute, but Sir Kruger quickly placed himself in front of Paul's face, letting him see the slimy raging hard-on. His dick was dripping grease and ass juice, swollen a deep red, ready to spill its hot load of cum into a hole, any orifice.

"See that slimy dick, boy?" Sir Kruger said. "It's going to shoot jism into your mouth real soon. You want that?"

"Yes, Sir, please . . ."

Before he could finish, the hot slippery dick was shoved into his mouth and forced all the way down his throat. Paul sucked and licked at the greasy meat, tasting grease and his own salty ass on the pumping sex weapon.

"Suck it!" the Master shouted, grabbing Paul's head and ramming his long pole in and out of the wet mouth.

Paul could feel the hot wet slime on his belly; his own dick was raging hard, gently squirming in the slippery confines between his sweaty belly and the slippery warm leather.

"Suck my big dick you worthless slave . . . you're just a

mouth for me to rape . . . an asshole for me to take . . ."

Paul sucked and swallowed the mantool, feeling the pressure in his own balls begin to build, realizing that he was about to shoot his load. Suddenly the Master pulled his cock out of Paul's throat and walked around behind him once again.

"I'm going to shoot it into your ass after all. I want to feel those hot shitwalls around my big prick . . ."

He sank his whole cock into the warm hole again, pumping furiously at once. The deep thrusts massaged Paul's tool against the wet table, and he knew that in a moment it would be here.

"Take it, slave, take it," Sir Kruger said, letting out a long low moan, pounding the horse-dick into Paul's ass, shoving it deeper and faster, feeling the aggressive masculine surge of power, the sensation of having an enormous penis twice its normal size, the wild high emotion of sudden hatred and love, a long moment of pure violence. And then, the sudden rush, a long moan, a yell, a loss of context, and all at once there was no slave, was no Master; there was only a man's cock and a man's ass fusing into a molten moment of pure male aggression, and as the burning cum shot spurts and spurts of hot liquid into the waiting ass, the two men became twice as masculine, twice as hard, twice as hot. The muscles, the sweat, the pulsing dicks, the flowing cum; all fused into a single act of creative aggression: mansex.

Completely spent, Sir Kruger climbed off Paul's ass, loosened his bonds, rubbed the raw wrists and ankles for a moment, and then left the chamber. Paul followed him out, found his way to the stairs, and began to ascend to the house above. Slowly Paul became aware of the storm, still blowing wild outside. The wind howled, and the rain was pouring heavily against the roof. He climbed the stairs, came out into the long candlelit hallway, and saw Sir Kruger standing there by the door. He smiled at Paul while he stood waiting, and Paul put his clothes back on.

Paul was ready to go, and he walked to the door. Sir Kruger smiled again, pulled Paul into his arms and kissed him. They embraced for a long moment, and then Sir Kruger said,

"Thanks, man."

"Yeah, thanks," Paul said. "Maybe we can do it again some-time . . ."

Sir Kruger smiled wryly, laughed and said, "You will return."

DEAR MASTER, DEAR SLAVE

D EAR SIR:
   Please, Sir, read this letter from a willing and obedient slave. I have seen You from far off for a long time, and i hope to serve You as slave if You find me worthy.

I exist only to service Your dick, in any way my Master chooses. I want very much to serve You, Sir, to kneel at Your feet and feel Your leather. At Your order i will strip in front of You and Your friends and kneel with my head down at Your feet.

You tell me to sit on the floor with my hands behind my back. You'll tie my wrists and warn me to keep my head down. Already my dick is hard from the opportunity to serve You. Suddenly i feel Your boot pressing on the head of my cock, forcing it to the floor. You press my cock into the floor, grinding Your boot against the thick manmeat.

You take Your foot away and order me to kneel and lick Your boots. I slide my tongue across the shiny black leather, polishing Your boots with my spit. You spit on my back as i kneel there, telling me how You're going to beat me and fuck me and piss all over me.

You take a leather hood that has only a mouth and nose opening and place it over my head. Now i am on my knees in front of you, my head in a hood, my hands tied behind my back. You order me to open my mouth and eat Your ass. I start to work my tongue on Your asshole, rimming around it, thrusting my tongue deep inside Your shit-chute.

You turn around and order me to suck Your balls, to lick them and take Your big ball sac in my mouth. I work Your balls over with my tongue and mouth, licking and sucking at Your man-sized globes.

Suddenly You shove Your prick in my mouth, fucking in and out of Your slave's willing mouth, feeling the warm soft interior of an obedient hungry throat. You pull out and tell me that You need to piss, that i'll be Your fucking urinal. You ask me if i want my Master's piss. I answer yes, Sir, i want You to piss on me. You ask me how much i want it, and i beg You, please, Sir, piss in my mouth, please let me drink Your hot yellow piss. You let go a steady stream of piss, squirting it all over my body, shooting piss on my cock and balls and then emptying Your bladder into my mouth while i eagerly swallow and drink all Your piss like the slave urinal that i am.

Now i'm dripping with piss, still tied and kneeling on the floor in a messy puddle of piss. You order me to stand, and You untie my hands, leaving me hooded and standing dripping wet in the middle of the room.

Suddenly i feel ankle restraints being wrapped around my ankles. You spread my legs and plant them about a yard apart from each other, securing them to steel rings in the floor. Next You attach wrist restraints and chains, and tie my arms up to the ceiling spread-eagled. You hoist my arms forward and up, so that i am hanging at a forward slant, just on the tips of my toes.

Now You start to work my tits, gently, teasingly at first, then firmer, rougher, pinching and tugging until I gasp in painpleasure. You clamp my tits with steel clamps, and then You hang weights from my tits.

Next I feel Your gloved hand passing over my balls, and You tell me that You're going to torture my little balls, going to squeeze them and stretch them out until i scream for mercy. I gasp as you seize them in Your firm leathered grip and wrench them up from behind me. You tug on them more, intermittently caressing them and then squeezing the shit out of them.

You wrap a ball stretcher around my ball sac and hang a weight from it. Now i'm hanging spread-eagled with weights dangling from my tits and nuts.

Soon You start to beat my ass with a paddle, slapping it up all red and hot. I beg You to fuck me, to shove anything up my hot, red ass. I feel Your gloved finger slide up inside my hole, slowly twisting and turning.

You ask me how much i want to be fucked, and i beg You, please, Sir, shove Your dick up my ass. You grease up a big fat dildo and press it against my tight, waiting asshole. I ask You to please shove it up my ass, and You twist it all the way, telling me what a fucking piss-drinking slave i am.

You fuck me with the dildo until i'm loose and begging for more. Then You take it out and put it in my mouth, gagging me with the big slimy dildo.

You untie me, take me down, and tie me up in the sling. I'm still hooded and i've got a dildo shoved in my mouth. I feel the head of Your cock pressed against my sloppy asshole, and then i feel the powerful thrust of Your hips as You ram Your throbbing hard-on deep into my greasy shithole. You fuck me hard, slapping Your belly against my balls until You feel the surge of cum flowing up and up and suddenly exploding inside my ass. You pump and slam and shoot Your heavy load, shouting about the worthless asshole i am.

You pull the dildo out of my mouth, free one of my hands, and order me to jerk off. You take me out of the sling and tell me to kneel and jerk off into a bowl on the floor while cleaning Your dick off with my tongue. I go to work on Your meat, licking it all over and tasting the last of Your cum, the grease, the ass juices. Just as i start to shoot my load, You piss on me again, and then You order me to drink my cum from the bowl.

I am waiting to serve,

a slave

Dear Slave:

Get a few things straight. You exist only to serve cock—as many and in as many different ways as I or any other man see fit.

You belong to dick; you are a possession of everyone with a cock. All of you is public property, every part of your body that gives you pleasure or pain is mine.

The rules are simple: you must obey. My body is the object of your worship, and my orders are to be swiftly obeyed. You may not stand in my presence; you may kneel, lie, or sit on the floor, but you may not stand. You may address me only as "Sir" or "Master." You are to be always available for my use.

At my order you will strip, removing all your clothes under my scrutinizing gaze. You kneel, head down, hands behind your back, awaiting my instructions. I walk around you, looking at your ass, your tits, your thickening prick. I reach out and pinch one of your tits, twisting it and tugging it up and away from your chest. You gasp in pain, but I order you to be silent for inspection. I order you to stand—excepting my own rule—so that your whole body is available for my look and touch.

My hand passes from your tit to your cock. I reach beneath it and grab your nuts, gathering them up in my hand. I squeeze them harder and harder, grabbing them firmly and holding you captive by your balls. I force my finger in your mouth while still holding your nuts in my other hand, telling you to get my finger good and wet. You suck on my finger with your mouth, getting it wet. I take it out and shove it up your ass, feeling the heat of your asshole, fucking it with my finger roughly while I yank on your balls in front.

I release you and order you to the floor on your back. You lie on the floor and I straddle your torso. You look up at me from below, at my leather chaps, at my leather vest, at my thick manmeat hanging heavy over your face.

I want to see you piss on yourself, and I order you to do so. You let your piss run out of your cock. It runs down your thighs, then you direct the stream of hot piss up on your stomach and chest. "Yes, you piss-slave," I say, "Look at you on the floor pissing on your own fucking self."

You stop pissing and I order you to get on your hands and knees. I kneel down and eat your ass, sticking my tongue up that chute, relaxing that hole. I grease up your hole, and then I shove a big black dildo up your ass, leaving it there.

"Get up, slave," I order, bringing you to your feet. The dildo is still stuck up your ass. I lead you to a sawhorse, bend you over it, and bind your hands and feet to the legs of the sawhorse. "Do you want your ass beaten, slave?" I ask. "Yes, Sir," you answer. "I can't hear you, dipshit!"

"Please, Sir, I beg you to beat my ass," you shout. "Okay, you asked for it," I say, and I haul off and whack your ass. You howl as the crack of my hand on your ass-flesh echoes in your sex chamber.

"Shut up, you goddamn piece of shit," I yell, yanking the greasy black dildo out of your ass and shoving it down your throat. I spank your ass, your ass-cheeks getting redder and hotter. You start to wiggle that hot ass, straining against your bonds to meet the palm of my hand as it soars in a fast line for your open ass.

I ask if your ass is horny, if you don't want a big fat dick up there. You shake your head yes, and when I pull the dildo out of your mouth you ask me to fuck you. "Please, Sir, fuck me." "Tell me exactly what you want, slave." I slap your ass again. "Sir, I want you to ram your prick up my tight ass." "How much?" "I'll do anything, Sir, please fuck me." I press the big head of my pulsing organ against your greasy asshole. You moan in anticipation—an indiscretion that earns you a slap on your already aching ass.

In one sudden thrust I force my hot meat up your backside. You cry out in pleasurepain as my burning eight-inch dick slides all the way up your upturned butt. I pull it out and spank your ass before plunging it up your butt again until my muscled belly slaps your reddened ass-cheeks.

I reach under and grab your balls, tugging backwards on them to draw your ass onto my fat tool. I stand behind you, my dick planted in your ass, and you fuck that hard pole every time I pull your ass onto it by your nuts. I thrust that stiff weapon up that slimy shit-hole, and with each ram I grip your sore gonads harder.

I yank my enormous sex out of your butt and walk around in

front of you. I pull the black dildo out of your mouth and shove my greasy hard-on down your throat. You suck and lick the hot ass-juices off my throbbing meat as I buck and thrust, driving my prick into your slurping mouth, fucking your face.

"You're a goddamn cocksucking piss-drinking slave, you shit-eating asshole, suck my big dick, man, suck that cock that just fucked your ass, suck it, man, get ready to drink my cum you motherfucking sonofabitch, swallow it!..."

You work your tongue around my organ while I shove it down your throat, and then I begin to moan and hold your head as my cum gathers and boils and gets ready to shoot into your sucking mouth. "You're just a hole, man, a soft hot place to stick my dick. Man, I'm gonna cum, I'm gonna shove this motherfucker down your throat and shoot my load. I'm cumming, man, cumming, drink it, swallow that stuff, cum..."

Suddenly you feel the violent contractions, and your mouth fills with my hot, sweet cum. You suck and swallow and milk my dick for more, and it keeps on pouring a steady pump of white love juice. You swallow it and lick my dick, and some of it drips out of your mouth.

Next you feel the hot stream of my piss on your cum-stained tongue, and you try to lap it up like a dog, like the piss-drinking urinal you are. I grab my dick and spray my hot piss in your face till your hair and moustache are dripping wet. I pick up a jockstrap off the floor and get it soaking wet with piss and rub it all over your face and body, like a washcloth soaked in piss.

I untie you and order you to wear the piss-soaked jock. You put it on, your hard-on straining against the cold jock, hoping for release, for orgasm. I order you to dress, to wear cowboy boots, a dog collar. I put wrist restraints on you, binding your hands together in front of you and push you out the door and into the truck in the street above.

A couple of guys walk by and see your restraints, see me in leather, and smile at what they know is the start of a hot evening. I stuff my jacket pockets with stuff for the night ahead, and then I drive us to the Caldron.

The Caldron is packed with hunky studs like always, dressed in tight jeans and leather. It's one of the busiest nights ever, and we cause quite a stir as I lead you up to the bar on a leash attached to your dog collar. I order you to strip down to the wet jockstrap. As you take off your jeans, the horny men around the bar take a good look at your bare ass and your piss-drenched jock. We check your clothes and I lead you to the tubs, forcing you to lie in the one in the back. Pretty soon three or four studs come up, pulling on their thick cocks, preparing to drench your body in piss. The most muscled stud, with a long, curving slab of horsemeat starts to shoot a steady stream of piss right into your mouth, and the other studs spray their hot beer piss all over your legs and chest, completely soaking your filthy jockstrap.

I lead you out of the tub and into the big room with slings. I lead you to the surgeon's table, lay you out flat, and peel off your dripping jockstrap. Several studs come over to watch as I stuff that filthy jockstrap in your mouth, gagging you to keep you silent for the next step.

I reach into my pockets and pull out a razor and a small bar of shaving soap. I order you to piss on the soap, and as you do, I lather up your cock and balls, getting your prick stiff. Slowly I begin to shave your cock and nuts, shearing them clean of every hair. Your naked cock sticks straight up like a rocket, and the shiny smooth globes of your balls glisten in the orange light.

The onlooking studs grin and nod their approval as I finish up and reach into my pocket, producing a pair of tit-clamps, a ball stretcher, and two lengths of chain.

I order you to the floor on your knees, telling you to crawl to one of the posts of the slings. I pull the jockstrap out of your mouth and position it on your head like a mask. You inch across the floor, your ass in the air, the jock on your head. A big stud in black boots and full leather steps in front of you and orders you to lick his boots. You spit-shine those boots and then you feel his hot piss spraying on your back. I order you to stand facing the corner post. I attach one of the tit clamps, then I run the chain around the post and attach the other clamp to your tit. I wrap the ball stretcher around your nut-sac, securing a chain from your balls around the post. You are now tied to the post by your tits and balls; you can move only about three inches without tugging tightly on your balls or your tits.

I invite the well-hung studmasters to have at it, and one by one you get fucked by big hard dicks, over and over, huge cocks pounding up your butt, slamming into your dripping asshole. One guy shoots inside you and is replaced by another throbbing prick. Cum drips out of your hole, running down your legs, making a puddle on the floor. More and more engorged sex weapons invade your slave hole, ramming deep inside you, pulling your body back, straining your tits, tugging your balls, and then a sudden heavy thrust will shove you up against the post, cutting into your swollen unsatisfied prick oozing a steady stream of pre-cum.

You're filled with hot loads from monster cocks pounding your hole. Studs stand around watching, jerking off, waiting for the opportunity to flood your sloppy hole with more burning cum. Harder and harder they ram their burning organs into your belly, telling you what a shit-eating slave you are.

Once you've been fucked by a couple dozen men, I let you loose, order you to kneel and lap up the puddle of cum on the floor, cum that drained out of your flooded rectum. You scramble to the floor, licking it shiny clean, tasting the mixed cum of so many studs. I order you to lie atop the long black platform behind the slings in the middle of the room, telling you to jerk off. You begin to pump your dick with your fist, with men walking by watching, and when you finally cum, I catch the hot spunk in my hand, bring it up to your face, rub your cum all over your face, pouring it into your mouth, and making you lick my hand clean. I lick your face clean of cum and wait to see what's next.

I am waiting to dominate.

A Master

THE SEX PIT

H E KNEW HE WANTED something more, something very different, something that would set apart this night in the vast history of his sexual experience. But he did not know how — or where — to find it. He had made the rounds of bars, baths, clubs, private orgies. He had indulged himself in countless savage ruttings with the men and women around him, but at that moment in time — a mysterious cross between summer and winter — his body and his imagination ached for something more.

And so, in the stillness of a strangely warm evening just beyond the autumnal equinox, he donned his sex garb and set out to discover what could be more bizarre, more challenging than he had already tried. He stretched his arms and back muscles as he pulled the stained tank top over his head and felt the soft cotton slide and stretch over his thickly muscled torso. He felt the last brush of air on his swaying cock before he stuffed it down the right leg of his tight, worn jeans. He laced the high black boots, wrapped the black leather armband around his left arm, pulled the motorcycle jacket on, zipped it up, and put on his heavy leather gloves.

It had often been like this, the relentless tugging at the back of his mind, the insistent images creating themselves in his imagination, forcing him out the door and into the dark. He knew the source, the wellspring of his passion — an undeniable

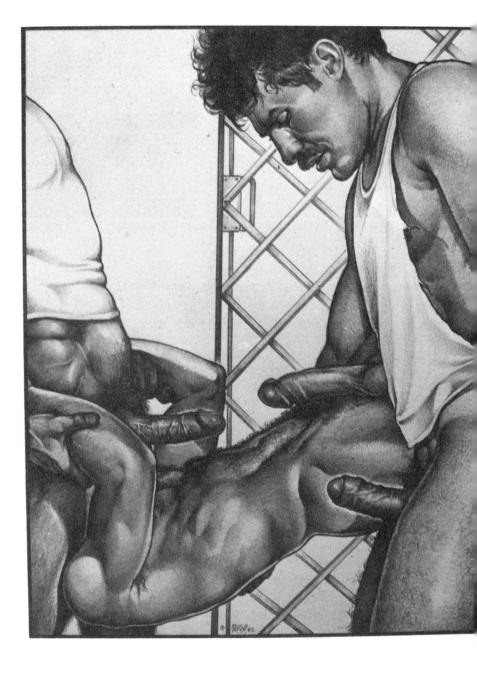

urge to press outward toward greater challenge, deeper pleasure. It was, at the essence, his way of destroying inhibition, of overcoming all constraints, and so he turned to go.

He was ready for sex. He was ready to find anything and anyone and use them, vilely if necessary, to satisfy his body, to still the demands of his manhood, his stiff rod. He climbed onto his motorcycle and headed for the waterfront, knowing full well what awaited him there.

And it was there. The men in leather, in torn blue jeans, in jocks, all cruising and groping and reaching out in exquisite and agonized lust for another man, another big dick, another set of hard muscles to pound and possess and destroy. It was intoxicating, this addictive mansex that drew these studs to this abandoned place and led them to the edge of their lust.

It was long past dusk but long before dawn, a time of night that knew no pressing boundaries. Infinite darkness stretched before and after the moment he arrived, seducing him into a lulled sense of time, when his cock could be satisfied over and over again, in any way that he desired.

The usual connections were possible—fucking, sucking, fisting, drugs, threesomes, foursomes, moresomes. But the insistent urge to go further, to the bizarre, drew him away, searching, looking, wondering. A sudden cool breeze chilled him, sent a shudder through his body, and in that instant he felt something akin to the other world; he was transported for only a moment, but in that moment he felt that there was something bizarre drawing him in.

Hours passed in mild lust, and even as he caught notions of the time from passing watches and whispered voices answering questions, he knew that time remained to find the unusual. And finally, in the middle of the night, a man leaned close, bent to his ear, and told him of the place, the place called The Pit.

"It is not a bar, it is not a club. Neither is it a bathhouse. It exists in the joint basement of two mansions, and it exists, in large part, in the minds of its participants. Here is the card, it is all you will need."

He was handed a plain black card, on which, in red lettering, was printed an address. It was the horrible section of town, an ancient abandoned region of bygone entrepreneurs. He turned to ask the man for more information, but as he turned and opened his mouth to speak, he saw that the man had gone. He knew that this was it, the mystery of which he had been precognizant earlier when the cold breeze had chilled him by the waterfront. He left on his motorcycle, arriving there within an hour. The area was deserted, but the address proved correct. He stood facing two enormous brick and marble mansions, crumbling, defeated, windowless. He reached for the card, ascended the crumbling stone steps, faced a huge oak door, and knocked.

He stood there and waited, then slowly the door opened. Standing there was a beautiful young man, heavily muscled, glistening with oil rubbed shiny over his nude body. The slave boy stood proudly, his neck encircled with heavy chain, his right tit pierced. The boy held out his hand to receive the black and red card, then retreated, beckoning that he should enter.

He walked into a grand foyer, covered with dust and debris. Cobwebs wove hideous patterns in broken chandeliers, and once-elegant rugs were torn, tattered, reeking of age and urine and rot. The boy walked forward, never looking back, leading him down two, possibly three levels, until he found himself in a small chamber. The boy vanished through a heavy blood-red drape, and he forced his way through the heavy fabric, entering a world that seemed fashioned from Dante's *Inferno*.

The room was a huge, vaulted chamber. Enormous braziers were scattered about the hall, burning with fires that illuminated the chamber. Set about the stone walls were standards of fire, torches burning bright, flooding the room with a sinsister red glow. The place resembled hell, and all at once he took in the heavy aroma of sex, the dark sensuous appeal of the fires, the torches, the vast chamber filled with nothing but exquisite men, all of whom were engaged in one form or another of sexual torture.

He entered the place more deeply, step by step, his lustful eyes consuming every male form, every sexual torture in action, every available slave chained to the wall or floor. He passed beneath a glowing brazier twice his height, to the other wall, which opened in several places into dim halls leading downward and beyond. He paced full circle around the vast chamber, watching as handsome leatherclad studs administered beautiful tortures to chained young men. He witnessed the piercing of a young man's tit, the gold ring sliding effortlessly through the tender flesh.

Then suddenly he came face to face with a tall, handsome man wearing nothing but a cock ring around his incredibly oversized cock and balls. "Welcome," the man said. The only sound that carried above the man's booming voice was that of whips cracking against flesh, and the dull background crackle of flames burning.

"There are no rules here, save those that spare lives. The slaves are here for your use—any of them, in any way you desire."

He acknowledged the short speech with a nod, thinking of several questions to ask the tall man, but before he could speak the man walked away. Then his attention was drawn to the lustful moans of a young man being fucked by two big dicks in the middle of the room. The slave was suspended from the ceiling, his ass spread wide as his legs were tied far apart. Two masters stood fucking him—one in front, one behind, ramming both their swollen pricks into the slave with ferocious vigor.

He watched for several minutes, then, in a sudden realization of his opportunity, he began to search the room for some slave into which to relieve his own sexual tension. He found an exquisite blond slave bound by the neck to the stone wall. He walked up to the boy and stared at him, then reached down and fondled the slave's tits, squeezing, pinching, and twisting until the boy began to wince.

He nudged the boy's cock and balls with his leather boot, pressing the genitals down, then hauling back his boot and kicking the heavy ball sac, kicking again and again until the slave's huge cock stood out firm and erect, the evidence of his servitude.

He rewarded the slave by shoving his sweaty prick into the eager mouth. The slave sucked and slurped, all the while enduring the constant torture of his tits and balls. He rammed harder and faster. The slave moaned in ecstasy as his tits were wrenched and his throat raped. In no time the cum boiled up, churning the length of his huge dick and flowing in hot steady spurts into the slave's tight throat. The slave sucked and swallowed eagerly, satisfied to serve this new master. The jism overflowed his mouth and dripped down his chin onto his chest and over his bruised tits.

When he was done with the boy, he left him and began to wander around the room. Just as he was about to find another slave to fuck, the tall handsome man reappeared with the oiled slave boy. Also with them were a half dozen other equally tall, muscular men, wearing nothing but chaps and leather boots. They began to strip, and then they stood before him wearing nothing but cock rings.

"You have been chosen," the man said. "We would like to see you perform as a bottom in our chamber of horrors, as this is called."

"But . . ." he began to protest.

"We realize that you consider yourself a top, but as I said, there are no rules here, no limits whatsoever." He could not protest, for at once the six naked men grasped his arms and legs and carried him to a frame constructed of heavy beams. They strapped him into it, more or less spread-eagled, but with his legs raised slightly and his head lowered. His torso was secured by leather straps so that he could not move.

Then they stripped him naked, tore his tank-top off, ripped and shredded his jeans, exposing his muscular body, his long, thick cock, his tight ass, his small, sensitive nipples.

"Very nice," the tall man said and took up a whip. The other men positioned themselves around him stroking their huge sex-weapons as they watched in anticipation. The tall man lifted the whip.

It fell through the dark air, slicing a path through the warm sex chamber as it lashed hard across his chest. He cried out as the huge monster raised the whip once more, letting fly the leather lash against his stripped body. The lash stung his prick and his balls, causing a dull ache to stab his groin, but his huge cock throbbed, oozing clear pre-cum to the floor.

Suddenly the whipping stopped. He was able to regain his senses for a moment and consider his predicament. He had not expected to be tied helplessly to a great wooden rack, his ass and cock and balls stuck up in the air under the scrutiny of half a dozen huge naked men.

Before he could think further, the group of musclemen grasped the rack and turned it over, exposing his ass and back to the whipmaster. "Ready for more?" was all the man said before he began to whip the hell out of the bound man. His ass tightened as the lash fell across his pale ass which grew red with welts. The pain was incredible, yet somehow strangely satisfying.

As quickly as it had begun, the whipping stopped. Two of the men unbound his ankles and wrists and brought him to a standing position while holding tight to his arms. The tallest man looked him over. "It would appear that you enjoy this, topman," he said, reaching down and roughly fondling his hard cock. He reached beneath the monster dick and grasped the heavy, low-hanging balls.

He did not move as the big strong hand closed around his nuts. The pain in his groin was agonizing as the fist clenched onto his balls and began to tug, pulling up and towards the ceiling. The two studs continued to grasp his arms, holding him in place but leaving his legs free. The tall leader pulled firmly on the giant nuts; the pressure pulled the ball sac tight.

"Oh . . ." he cried out as his feet were lifted off the floor, his arms held tight by the studs, his legs rising from the floor as the tall man pulled at his balls.

"Enough," the big man said, letting go of the balls and letting his feet fall to the floor. "Let's continue."

With that, the six men grabbed him again, dragged him to a leather sling, and tied him tightly into it. Without hesitation the big men began to torture him. They secured tit clamps to his nipples. They strapped a ball stretcher to his sore nuts, then attached a heavy weight to the stretcher, pulling painfully on his balls.

Before he knew what was happening, he was being force-fed a tab of acid. Then he was left alone for a short while. He hung there in the sling, tits aching and nuts churning from the torture devices attached to them. He relaxed in the drug; the sounds changed vaguely, indistinctly. A distant cry of a slave in painpleasure flew around the stone chamber, and he could see the sound travel in circles around the room, flirting with the flames of the torches.

He glanced at the flames, which leapt and danced; then he made out—in the distance, it seemed—a group of huge men converging on him, enclosing him from all angles, enveloping him in a total multiple masculinity.

He was aware of a swarm of astounding strength and aggression converging on his form, groping, grabbing, slapping, hitting, biting, pinching, demanding. The scene grew and expanded. Piss flew into his mouth from huge curved dicks hanging heavy over his face, pointing their hot streams into his open mouth. Then those same huge cocks lowered themselves into his mouth, forcing it wide open, forcing their way deep into his throat.

They shifted, became hot steaming assholes, manholes sitting on his face, his tongue sliding deep inside the velvety hot rectums. They slid on and off his face, in and out of his mouth. His tongue worked constantly on cocks and big balls, greasy buttholes aching to be bathed with spit and a warm tongue.

He was a receptacle, a big loose hole where the musclemen laid their dicks, where huge fat pricks could slide inside and fuck, ramming into his slippery ass, now slick with great gobs of lube. The men took turns slamming their throbbing cocks deep inside him; his ass was rewarded with squirts of burning cum, which someone would suck out of his hole and feed back to him in a vicious kiss.

They became a sexual unit, became sex itself. There was nothing in that chamber but muscle and cock and semen, and it was all congruous with him, connected to his own throbbing dick which, now in the heat of the pounding and sucking and licking, began to quiver, to tremble with tortured pain and hesitation. His bound balls ached as his ass ground against whatever huge organ was embedded in it. Slowly, quickly, agonizingly, the hot juices began to boil, and he passed over the edge into a deep void of knowing that something had to happen.

He yelled out when the moment came. He knew that three, four, seven men were cumming, were coating his enslaved body with burning man-liquid. He opened his mouth wide, tasting the white fluid, tasting the sweet-salty juice of masculinity, while his own cock lurched and jumped and squirted great spurts, dropping heavy hot globs on his belly.

Then he slept and dreamed. He dreamed of men and pain, of torches and piercings, of long uncut cocks dripping piss and cum, of wide muscular chests covered with sweat and urine. When he awoke he was unbound and lying by the heavy red curtain where he had entered.

He had no idea of the passage of time. Had he been drugged for an hour? More? Less? He saw that he was once again wearing jeans and a shirt, though they were not his own. His motorcycle jacket was there, and his boots and gloves.

He left the place, climbing the flights of stairs to the rotting foyer above. He drew open the heavy wooden door, and the harsh sunlight blinded him. He walked out. His motorcycle was still there, although it had been moved beneath a sort of shed.

He walked over to it and stopped short. The motorcycle was covered with dust, as though it had stood for quite some time. He climbed aboard to fire up the engine, discovered it to be sluggish, as if the battery were weak. He wiped his finger across the metal. The dust was very thick. The cycle had obviously been sitting for quite some time.

He frowned. How long was I here? he thought. How long?

COWPOKED

I GREW UP IN YOSEMITE National Park, in California, where my father was a forest ranger and my mother worked for the National Park system. We had a little house there, and I went to school some miles away. Every couple of months we'd take a drive down into the valley and over to San Francisco to visit my grandparents, who lived in a tall, grim Victorian in the Western Addition.

Those two realities—Yosemite and San Francisco—had something to do, I'm sure, with my present life and orientation. I still live in Yosemite part of the year—when I stay with my folks. The rest of the year I live in San Francisco, where I run my own business.

Every summer I take off for the High Sierra again, usually staying at my folks' place in Yosemite Valley for a month before striking out into the backcountry for a month or two on the trail, away from civilization.

That's what I did this summer. It was the tenth time I've done so since moving to San Francisco at the age of eighteen. I spent the first month at my folks' house, relaxing, hiking, and rock climbing. But this year, for the first time, I found something different.

I was out for a long hike around the valley floor in Yosemite on a hot June afternoon. A cool breeze was beginning to stir through the pines, softening the heat. I could hear the steady rumble of the falls and the rushing stream of the Merced River as I plodded along. Pretty soon I found myself at the stables, watching the cowboys throw out hay for the horses and mules.

When I was little, I used to come and stand just like that at the stables, my little boy's hands grasping the wooden rails of one of the stable fences, my little boy eyes drinking in the sight of the tough, brawny young men in worn, tight jeans, boots, and cowboy hats. They were always spitting tobacco juice, and I remember how I used to imitate them, spitting on the ground until my mother would catch me and tell me in no uncertain terms to *cut that out*.

Now, twenty years later, I was standing there again staring at the cowboys, who were still the same youthful sort of men. But now we were all near the same age. I guess the park employs young cowboys from Wyoming and Montana, so there's a constant influx of young men, year after year.

One cowboy really caught my eye. Short and stocky, with arms about as thick as my legs, he had a dark, bristly moustache. As he threw the hay out with a pitchfork, I watched his thick biceps bulge up into a big round knot, then lengthen again as his arms extended to pitch the hay. He was packed in tight in his western wear. Every move pushed his thick butt against the seat of his jeans, and I could see his thick chest muscles straining his tight plaid shirt. His pocket outlined the round can of chewing tobacco, and I could see a belt with his name stitched on the back: JACK. Well, I thought to myself, you couldn't get more simple, western, or masculine than "Jack."

I kept on looking, watching the dark sweat stains under his arms get bigger. There was also a triangular patch of sweat on the back of his shirt, disappearing into his jeans. I wondered what it would be like to lift his shirt tail and lower his jeans, searching for the telltale mustiness of his sweat and hard work. My short reverie on this subject made my own jeans start bulging, as my dick lengthened and fattened.

Needless to say, he noticed me noticing him. He had stopped for a moment to wipe his forehead with his bandana—dark

blue, if it matters—and he glanced over at me. My right leg
was planted on the lower rail of the fence, my arms were crossed
and supporting me as I leaned against the top rung of the
wooden stable fence. He nodded and smiled, then spat. I
nodded and smiled, kind of nonchalant—I didn't want him to
get ornery if I had him sized up wrong.

But of course I wasn't wrong. He kept looking back as he
worked at the hay. He'd stop and glance over at me, then
resume his work. It wasn't very long—maybe two or three
minutes—until he finally drove the pitchfork into the ground
and swaggered over my way.

My heart pumped hard as the muscled cowboy walked my
way, but I just stood there leaning against the fence, cool and
easy. He came up to me and spat again, then fixed me with a
long, cool stare.

"Howdy," he finally said. "Out for a walk?"

"Yep," I answered. "I live here, just out for the afternoon."

"Live here?" he said, raising his eyebrows and spitting once
again.

"Sure; I grew up here. During the winter I live in San Francisco, but come summer, I'm back to stay with the folks before
heading up into the high country for some backpacking."

He nodded, then looked away. His eye was fixed on a mare
prancing around on the other side of the stables. He kept watching the horse, then said: "San Francisco, huh?"

"San Francisco," I affirmed, knowing exactly what he meant.

"Nice town," he said. "But I ain't much into big cities." He
spat again, still gazing intently at the mare. "But I get down
there now and again for weekends, ya know . . ." He let this
remark out soft, as if implying more than he said.

"Of course," I answered, knowing again exactly what he
meant. "That's why I live there."

He nodded and grinned, looking back at me and extending
his hand. "Jack," we both said at once, as he introduced himself. "I read your belt," I explained. He nodded again, still
grinning.

"Damn hot out here," the cowboy said, running his hand

across his sweaty forehead. I could see the big sweat stains under his arms, and when he lifted them, I could smell the sweet raunch of his armpits.

"Sure is," I agreed, feeling the bulge in my pants get even bigger.

"How 'bout getting some shade?" he said, looking across at one of the stable houses.

I nearly froze up at the immediacy of his invitation. I had thought I might have to work at seducing this cowboy, but here he was, coming on as big as day. "You bet," I answered, and together we started to walk along the length of the fence—he on one side, I on the other—until we reached the gate. He opened it and let me into the stable, and we started to walk across the hay and dirt towards the barn.

Just as we neared the barn door, he reached up and slapped me on the back, a strange, fraternal gesture that confused me for a moment. But then he kept his hand there on my back and used it to propel me through the door, into the warm, dusty interior. The light was murky—it filtered dimly through cracks in the wood, and the place smelled of hay and manure, dust and horseflesh. It was an aphrodisiac, that smell. His hand remained planted on my back, propelling me further into the dim interior of the barn. He pushed me into one of the horse stalls filled with hay.

I could hardly believe the scene was really happening. It was too much like a fantasy, but then, why not? I was at home in Yosemite, with a young hot cowboy, and we had slipped into a barn for a fuck. What could be more simple?

He pushed me down into the pile of hay and dropped on top of me, locking his lips onto mine and thrusting his tongue into my hungry mouth. Our tongues played, the tips met and dueled, our lips brushed. He ran his tongue over my lips, then bit my lower one, finally nibbling and sucking on the tip of my tongue. I felt the bulge in his jeans against my leg; the bulge in my own jeans strained to break free.

I buried my face in his armpit, in the damp shirt, sniffing and enjoying the strong, honest odor. I moved my hands across his chest and began to unbutton his shirt. Finally I got it off and saw his nude torso—thick, tan, covered with hair and sweat. I plunged into his armpit again, lapped at the raunchy hair, soaked it with my spit as I licked his salty sweat.

He fumbled with his belt buckle, unbuttoned his jeans, and took them off along with his boots while I continued to lick his armpits. He pulled my face back to his and kissed me again, tasting his own sweat on my lips and tongue. When I reached down between us to feel his erection, I gasped at the enormity of what I felt. It was the way I imagined it: long and tremendously thick. It was the thickness that was shocking; the monstrous thing must have been as thick as a coke bottle, and his balls, which hung down heavy in a long sac, were about the size of apricots. I grabbed them and squeezed, and he responded with a moan of lust. I reached up to his erect nipples and tugged on them as well. He moaned his pleasure again.

He stripped me, pulling my clothes off rapidly. When he saw my cock thrust proudly up and my big balls hanging between my legs, he let out a low whistle. "Fucking monster," he said, staring down at my dick and wrapping his fist around it. "Fucking tool," he said, pumping my huge cock in his fist.

Before I knew what was happening, he shifted position and straddled my torso, bringing his ass over my face. I stayed on my back and he knelt forward, sliding my hard dick into his mouth and lowering his sweaty, musty asshole onto my mouth. I eagerly ate his ass out, licking at the sweat, probing the tight hole with my hot tongue.

His mouth slipped up and down on my hard pole; I was amazed at his facility. This hunky cowboy had my whole fucking dick down his throat, and he was milking it with his mouth and tongue. His asshole on my mouth was growing loose and slippery; I began to feel as though I'd like to fuck this hot cowboy number.

And so I raised myself and slapped his ass. It was hard—two perfectly round little mounds of thick muscle, with an inviting crack and hot hole between. I pushed him down, shoved his shoulders into the hay, and raised his hips to crotch level as I got on my knees. He loved it, started to beg for it.

And I gave it to him. In the dark barn, with the sweaty muscled cowboy bent forward in front of me, his muscled ass stuck up in the air towards my dick, I took a deep breath—smelling the hay and manure—and stuck my cock against his hole. He begged for it, so I shoved it in, his loose wet hole facilitating my smooth entry.

As soon as my huge dick was embedded in his butt, I started to fuck him with fast long motions, ramming it in and out hard. His hips thrust back to meet my insistent plunges, and the sight of it all—the hot cowboy in front of me, my big dick ramming in and out of his ass—brought me to the point of orgasm in a few minutes.

I pulled out my bloated dick, now shiny with assjuice and cum, and rolled him over on his back. His monster dick stood imperiously out from his flat belly, and my fist closed around it, pumping. With my other hand I grabbed his balls and started to tug on them mercilessly. I shoved my slick dick into his mouth and told him to clean it off while I stroked his dick. Within a minute or two he was breathing heavy, his mouth slurping at my cock, his huge sextool ready to explode in my fist, his swollen balls twisted and pained in my other iron-fist.

He screamed out when his dick erupted in huge spurts, but my dick in his mouth gagged the sound. Wave after wave of hot cum squirted up over his belly, down over my hand, until at last he was spent.

We lay back in the hay, panting, trying to recover our normal breathing. "Got myself a partner for the summer," I said idly.

"Sure do," he agreed. Outside, the mare neighed and galloped around the stables.

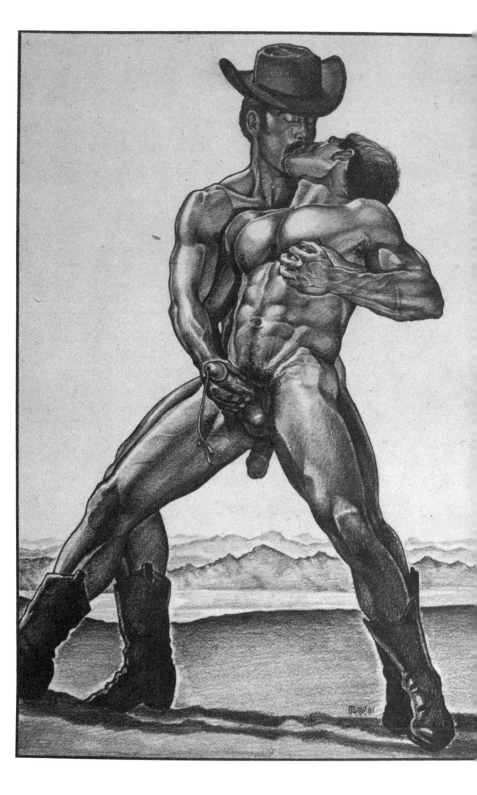

BREAKIN' IN AT THE RODEO

W HENEVER THE RODEO COWBOYS rode saddle bronc, Montana Jackson always waited on the edge of his seat to hear the whistle blow. For Montana, saddle bronc riding was the most exciting. He'd tense up watching the cowboy hold on tight, his strong arm wrapped up in the short rope, his other strong arm deliberately moving up and down to maintain balance. A good, long, controlled ride was always a good thrill to watch.

When the saddle bronc riding was done, Montana got up and went to the refreshment stand to get another beer. He spent the rest of the afternoon watching the bull riding, calf roping, and finally, the girl's barrel racing, always the last event of the day. Dust rose in the arena, Montana swallowed the last of his beer, and the sun began to set, casting a brilliant red glow across the far span of the horizon. This was Wyoming, a helluva beautiful place, he thought to himself.

Folks started to leave the grandstands, picking up their ice chests and pillows and jackets, rushing out to their pick-ups so they could hit the bars and restaurants downtown. Montana felt restless, though. He wasn't ready to go home, so he bought another beer and took a stroll around the arena.

The rodeo clowns were rolling the barrels onto the back of a pickup, contestants were gathering up their gear and tack, heading for the road and the next rodeo. Montana just sauntered around, eventually leaving the arena and walking back by the stables and barns.

"Hey, rascal," he said, as he reached through the slats in the stable fence to pat the neck of a sorrel stallion. The horse nudged his hand, letting out a friendly snort. Montana watched the stallion move away, break into a gallop, and circle around the stable. Montana looked around and started walking aimlessly beyond the stables, in the direction of some barns and other old buildings. He glanced inside one of the barns. A young cowboy was grooming a gorgeous chestnut mare, rubbing the horse's flanks with a rough towel. The cowboy looked up at Montana, said howdy, and then turned back to his work. Montana continued on, further into the dark between the old barns and enclosed stables. He noticed that only two of the larger barns in front were actually in use. Further away from the arena and the grandstands, some rickety barns and stables stood empty and dark, like big black boxes set against the deep purple of the gathering night.

Montana poured the rest of his beer down his throat, crumpling the can and tossing it aside. He continued to walk towards the old buildings, looking around and enjoying the warm spring air of early evening.

Just as he had nearly reached the last of the abandoned barns, he thought he heard someone say something. He stopped and looked around, but nobody was anywhere to be seen. Intrigued, Montana moved close to the old barn, listening to his own breathing. As he stood there, he was pretty sure that he heard some scuffling noises inside, and the sound of distant, muted voices. It sounded like a party, or maybe a fight; he couldn't tell. He walked along the wall, looking for a crack or door to look inside.

He found an open place where one of the boards had come loose. He peered into the darkness of the barn, but all he could make out was a dim light coming from somewhere on the other side of the barn. He circled round, being very careful now, as the voices continued in a gruff, but almost laughing way. Suddenly he came to an open door. He looked in and saw that the light was coming from a room inside the barn. He walked into the barn and moved around a wall until he could see the entrance to the interior room. The door was ajar, and Montana could see that it was lit rather dimly by an old lantern hanging in one corner. Montana wasn't prepared for what he saw next.

Hanging from the center of the room was a young, blond cowboy. He was tied spread-eagled, suspended from a beam in the ceiling so that his feet were about six inches from the straw and sawdust covered floor. The rope was wrapped around his wrists and then secured over the beam and fastened to big eye hooks in the walls. His ankles were bound by ropes that pulled his legs apart; these ropes were also fastened to the two walls. The kid wore a red bandana around his neck, and someone had blindfolded him with a black bandana.

Montana heard voices coming from the far end of the room. "Doesn't he look fucking good up there like that?" Another man said, "Yeah, he sure does; he looks like he's all ready for some use, man, looks like he's just waiting for us to go to work on him."

Obviously, the two hunky cowboys were satisfied with their handiwork. They must have just strung the guy up, and now were standing back for a moment to have a look at their helpless cowboy-slave, all tied up and blindfolded and ready to be used for their sadistic sexual pleasures.

Montana thought the scene was damn horny. He was a man who always knew what he wanted, and he always got it. All his life he'd wanted men, and all his life he'd gotten them. Ever since he was a little boy growing up near Cheyenne, he'd been interested in men, the more hunky and masculine, the better. Since then, he'd been around—the circuit—New York, Chicago, San Francisco, Key West. He'd even been to Berlin once, to get his fill of heavy-duty mansex. Now he was back in Wyoming, living on the ranch. He had a few other gay cowboy friends in Wyoming, but as he saw these two guys move into view, he didn't recognize them.

One of them wore a pair of Wrangler jeans, cowboy boots, and a plaid shirt open down the front. He was drinking a tall beer and circling around the spread-eagle suspended slave boy.

The other cowboy was really chunky, thick muscles rippling in his huge arms, a thick well-defined chest covered with dark hair. He wore nothing but a pair of brown western chaps, fringed with suede, and a pair of elephant-ear cowboy boots. He swigged on a long beer, too, and then spoke to the boy.

"Whatta you think of that, cowpoke? Ya like being up there, fucking helpless?"

The kid nodded. The cowboy splashed beer up into the kid's face, soaking the black blindfold. "Listen, brat, when your fucking cowboy masters speak to you, you answer with a loud and clear, Yes Sir!"

The kid said, "Yes, Sir," at once.

"That's better," the muscular cowboy said. "We don't ever want to hear you say No, because all we want is to hear Yes, Yes, Yes. Because everything we want you to do, or everything we want to do to you is to be fully submitted to. You understand?"

"Yes, Sir!" the bound slave answered.

The muscular cowboy walked up to the hanging body and ran his hand down the back, over the smooth blond ass, down along the back of the strong thigh, around to the front of the leg, up to his stomach, chest, shoulders, arms. The slave shuddered in pleasure as the cowboy's rough hands passed lightly over his body. Suddenly the cowboy reached out with both hands and pinched the kid's tits, wrenching them and twisting them until a gasp was forced out of the boy. He continued to pinch one tit, while bringing his other hand down to the boy's balls.

He wrapped his hand firmly around the dangling ball sac. The kid's balls were big, like oranges, and his scrotum hung low in the open air between his spread and tied legs. The hunky dude pinched the tit and tugged on the balls really hard. The kid cowboy tried to wriggle his body away from the painful grasp, but it was no use; there was no place for him to go. He was completely at the mercy of these two cowboy masters and was going to have to take whatever they decided to dish out.

"Take it, slave," the cowboy ordered as he continued to pull on those big globes, stretching the ball sac down and away from between those legs. "C'mon and take it; show us how much of a cowboy you are. Are you fucking masculine enough to service two dudes? Are you?"

"Yes Sir," the kid answered. "Please, sir, let me prove how much of a man I am."

"Okay, kid," he said. "Just remember, you asked for it."

Just then the cowboy in the plaid shirt came forward with a length of rough rope. The hunky dude let go of the kid's tit and balls, letting them flop freely again in the vulnerable space. The hunky cowboy moved around behind the boy and began to run his hand over and around the tight blond ass and narrow hips. In front, the other cowboy was making a hangman's noose, only small. As the hunky cowboy fingered the kid's ass, the cowboy in front fitted the noose over the big balls, pulled it tight, and then let the rope dangle there, hanging from the ball sac pulled tight by the noose.

"You like that, eh?" he said. The slave said, "Yes, Sir."

"What else do you like? You feel my friend's hand back there, playing with your tight little ass? You fucking better like it, because that hole's going to give us some use tonight. Ain't that right, Mat?"

"Sure is, Tom. We're going to have a field day with this little thing. It's as tight as a goddamn beer bottle or something."

As he finished his remark, he roughly shoved his middle finger into the tiny asshole. The slave let out a gasp, but cowboy Tom yanked on the rope between the kid's legs, causing a sharp pain in his balls that distracted him completely from the rough fat finger penetrating his tight asshole.

"Yeah, boy, that's good. You can gasp a little bit now and then, just to let us know you appreciate the treatment. But no more than that. We don't want to hear no crying or pleas for goddamn mercy."

As Montana watched, he knew that he couldn't just stand there all night with a raging hard-on, watching these two beautiful men work that pretty little cowboy. His eight-inch tool was already straining at his jeans, and he had absent-mindedly started rubbing it. He noticed that there was a transistor radio playing country music quietly somewhere in the room. In the distance he could hear Patti Smith crooning some heartbroken story of a lost man.

"Yeah, man, that hole is loosening up real good," Mat said, as he finger fucked the boy. "That's gonna feel real good wrapped around my big cock. You want that, kid?"

"Yes, Sir."

"Yes Sir what?" Tom barked, giving a rough yank on the bound balls.

"Yes Sir I want your dick in my ass."

"You'll get it, don't worry," Tom said. "You'll get it from both of us, soon enough."

Just then cowboy Mat shoved two more fingers into the asshole, now starting to drip clear ass juice, getting lubricated by the constant in and out motion of the cowboy's finger. When he shoved two more fingers in, though, the kid tried to raise his hips somehow, to try to avoid the invading thick fingers.

Mat ignored this, but nodded to Tom who took the end of the rope and walked forward, pulling the boy's balls forward, stretching them out as far as they would go. The two big orbs were pulled right to the bottom of the big ball sac. They looked round and shiny pulled out in front of him by the rope. Tom fastened the rope to a slat in the wall. Now the kid was suspended by arms and legs, and his balls were securely tied to the wall. He couldn't move his ass much now.

Mat finger fucked the kid and said, "Now see, boy, we got you all fixed up so you can't get away with that shit. Your ass is for us, man, and we don't want you thinking you can go and move it away from our fucking big dicks." Suddenly Mat pulled his fingers out, spread the ass-cheeks apart, and dived in with his tongue. The boy let out a long, low moan of pleasure at having his raw stretched hole bathed with warm spit by a long soft tongue. Mat licked and sucked, shoving his hot tongue up inside the open shit-chute, flooding the slave with spit and with incredible pleasure.

In front, Tom decided it was time to have a little more fun. He picked up his beer off the floor and poured it on the kid's chest, his tits dripping the yellow fluid, and he poured the cold beer all over the boy's sizable dick and balls. The kid's cock was about seven inches long, but it was really thick, with a big shiny head. His hard-on pointed up towards his belly, since his balls were pulled so far forward.

Mat kept on licking and sucking the ass, preparing it for the invasion soon to come, and Tom poured the rest of his beer on the kid's cock. The cold liquid diminished his hard-on just a bit, so Tom grabbed another length of rope and tied the half-hard cock down to the taut rope attached to the kid's big balls. As soon as the cowboy tied that dick down, it started to grow hard again, pressing against the three or four loops of rope tied around it. Tom knew that this was excruciating, but the warm tongue in the kid's asshole was providing him with a balance of actual pain and real pleasure.

Tom rummaged around the floor for a minute and found some tit clamps, butterfly clamps. "I got some tit clamps here, slave-boy," he told the bound kid. "I think I just might need to attach these."

As he said this, he clamped both tits at once, sending a mixed wave of pleasure and discomfort through the slave. Mat could tell it was working, because the kid's asshole suddenly tightened around his tongue, then opened up again.

"That looks real good," Tom said. "How does that feel, little cowboy?"

"It feels good, Sir."

"Yeah? Well it'll feel a little better here in just a second when I tie your little tits to that beam over your head." Tom grabbed the last of the rope and ran it through the clamps, pulling the tits up and away from the boy's chest. He threw the rope over the beam and then secured it to one of the ropes holding the boy's arms.

The kid was completely in bondage. His movement was restricted by the rope tugging at his cock and balls, as well as the rope pulling on his tits.

"Okay, kid, we're ready to use you," Tom said. Mat pulled his tongue away from the relaxed hole and placed a crate on the floor behind the kid. His big cock jutted out between his chaps, all swollen and purple, pulsing with thick veins and a foreskin now pulled back. He climbed up on the crate and placed his huge dick at the wet asshole. He rubbed it back over the hole.

"Feel that man's dickhead rubbing your asshole, slave?"

"Yes, Sir, I do."

"Know what a real cowboy's dick feels like when it's shoved up your ass?"

"No, Sir." Mat slapped the kid's ass.

"Never tell us no to anything shithead. Got that?"

"Yes, Sir. I'm sorry Sir." He was, too.

"Yeah, you're gonna want this big old monster dick thrust up inside you, huh?"

"Yes, Sir. Please Sir."

"Please, Sir, what?" Mat asked.

"Please, Sir, shove your man-sized cowboy prick inside me."

"Alright, kid, you're getting the idea, you're gonna feel this big dick sliding into your hot hole, inch by inch, and you're gonna swear it's that fucking stallion out in the corral."

Mat started to push his throbbing cockhead into the red-hot hole. The slave gasped, but Mat felt the kid's ass open up to take the huge hard-on. Tom stood back to watch, stripping off his shirt, jeans, and then putting just his boots on.

"Here it comes, kid, inch by inch," Mat said, and started to slide his cock inside the waiting boy-hole. "You know how long this thick thing is, boy?"

"Yes Sir."

"Oh yeah? How long?"

"Very long, Sir."

"Is that all you know?" Mat asked. "Well, little cowboy, this fucking monster that's sliding into your beggin' little hole is a full ten inches, and you've got about two inches inside you right now."

"Ooooooh," the slave moaned as more of the dick pushed into his ass.

"Four inches, five inches, six," Mat counted as he eased the throbbing pole into the velvet hot ass. With one final thrust he shoved the rest of his dick into the kid's belly, jamming his full thick ten inch man-meat into the deep hot shit-chute.

"Oh, yeah," Mat said, "that feels damn good in there."

"Looks good, too," Tom said, now stroking his own long pole to full erection. The slave moaned and tried to move his ass down onto the fabulous cock but the rope tied to his balls and tits prevented him from sucking more of the meat into his gut.

"I see what you want," Mat said, in response to the kid's attempt to fit more dick into his ass. "You just need a lot of good fucking from a giant stallion dick, don't you?"

"Don't You!" Tom shouted.

"Yes, Sir!" the slave obediently answered.

Mat pulled his dick all the way out and then thrust it all the way back in again, all in one violent motion.

"Oh, yeah," the slave whispered, lost in an ecstasy of being impaled helpless on a huge throbbing cock, unable to move without pulling his tits and balls to painful levels.

"Is this what you want?" Mat asked, as he shoved his cock hard into the hole again.

"Oh, yes Sir. I love that man-meat inside me."

With that encouragement, Mat sunk his full, thick ten inches into the ass, watching as the big dick disappeared into the wet hole. He started to pump with short, fast strokes, intermittently plowing the hole with one sudden big thrust. The kid fully relaxed and lost all tension, resting his limbs on the rope, no longer fighting the bondage, no longer fighting the invading cock, surrendering completely to the sensation of being fucked by a real man, a cowboy stud.

Then, as he moaned and groaned, Mat thrust his loins against the ass. His belly slapped up against the round, firm ass cheeks, and his wet cock made a raunchy, slurping sound as it plowed in and out of the cowpoke's hole. Mat shoved his dick deep into that ass, rubbing the prostate gland with the big round head of his dick, feeling the glorious sensation of the warm velvet ass walls clinging to his dick.

"Like it slave?" Mat managed to ask as he fucked harder and harder. The slave only moaned in response. Mat pumped harder and harder, shoving his huge pole in and out with as much force as he could. He shoved and groaned, and ground his belly against the ass, growling and plowing the tight hole, mercilessly pounding his fat dick in and out of the shit-chute, pumping and shoving deeper.

"Feel that big dick up there, boy?" he yelled. "Feel that horse dick fill you up?"

"Oh, yes Sir, I love it, Sir, please Sir, fuck me harder, fuck me the way you want; I want to prove I'm a man, I'm a cowboy; I can take it, please Sir, SHOVE IT UP MY ASS!"

Mat went crazy then, bucking his hips forward and ramming the fucktool deep into the slave boy. The kid ate it up, loving the hard mansex, and Mat began the gradual ascent to orgasm.

"Oh, yeah, cowboy, I'm gonna flood your useless ass with cum, man; you're gonna get a big fucking load of hot love juice shot way up inside you." He thrust harder. Sweat glistened on his muscular body. The hair on his chest was wet with sweat.

Drops of sweat fell from his forehead onto the kid's back. "Yeah, boy, you're gonna have so much cum inside you that you'll think you're getting a goddamn enema!"

Mat forgot to talk anymore as he approached the moment. He became an animal, a fucking sex machine, just one huge phallus forcing his way in and out of the surrendered asshole. He pounded harder, feeling an incredible tightness in his balls, feeling a huge contraction, a throbbing forward wave, an aggressive violent sudden movement of full force as his thick hot cum poured into the waiting belly, flooding the hot ass-chute with the burning white liquid, dumping his big load into the obedient cowboy, squeezing the last big drops of jism up into the deep hole.

"Whew!" Mat said, wiping the back of his hand across his forehead and shaking the wet drops onto the slave's back. "That was one helluva fuck!"

His big hard-on was still in the slave's ass, but with one sudden movement he pulled it out and looked down at his bloated, shiny dick, covered with shiny ass juice and cum.

"What a fuck!" Tom agreed, his own long pole still hard and unsatisfied.

Mat and Tom both turned toward the door when they heard a sneeze.

Montana stepped back from the door. Shit! he thought to himself, what a goddamn stupid wimpy thing to do. But before he could even turn in the darkness to run away, Tom grabbed his arms from behind. He pinned his arms back, Montana kicking wildly, but Mat grabbed his legs and helped Tom haul him into the hot room. Montana struggled to get free, but he started to give in, started to surrender himself to the two hunky cowboys who were holding him down on the floor. After all, this is what he liked, wasn't it? Some heavy mansex?

Montana went limp, lay on the floor, and looked up at the handsome men, his captors. Mat sat down on his stomach, pinning him to the floor. Tom climbed up on the crate, untied the black bandana blindfold, pulled it off the kid cowboy, and said:

"Take a look, kid, you got company."

Montana lay on the floor, pinned down by the heavy muscular cowboy. He looked up at the suspended slave boy looking down at him and noticed how blue his eyes were.

"Yeah, kid," Tom said to the slave, "you got some company here. Another hunky cowboy slave just dropped in." He laughed and stepped down next to Montana. Mat reached around to Montana's crotch, and what he found there told him that this stud was ready for some real mansex.

Montana wriggled beneath the muscular cowboy as he rubbed his hand over the bulge in Montana's jeans. Montana's dick was about eight inches long, thick, and when it was pent up in jeans made a big fucking lump down his right thigh.

"I think he likes this," Mat said to Tom, as he fingered the bulging cock. "I think he's gonna provide some real good use for us."

"Fucking A he is," Tom agreed.

Mat spit in Montana's face and said, "You wanna get fucked, cowboy? Wanna feel Tom's long dick up your ass?"

Montana said nothing; he lay motionless, a hint of fear registering in his eyes.

Mat spit in his face again, "Hey, fucker, answer me when I talk to you!"

Montana knew what to say. "Yes, Sir, fuck me." He felt a sudden rush of blood to his groin as he muttered the words, his thick manmeat straining for release.

"That's better," Tom said, grabbing Montana by the hair and pulling him up to a kneeling position. Tom placed his dick at Montana's lips and ordered: "Suck my fucking big dick, shithead, eat it all up."

Montana opened his mouth and darted his tongue to the head of the dick.

"I said suck it, not lick it," Tom said, spitting in his face. Montana opened his throat and slid his mouth down over the huge organ, swallowing the head in one long motion. Tom groaned in pleasure as the hot mouth slid over his dick, all the way to the black curly pubic hair.

As Montana continued to suck Tom's cock, Mat grabbed his arms and pinned them behind his back. He got a strap of leather and bound Montana's wrists to his elbows, so that his arms were completely restrained behind his back. Tom started to fuck his face, sliding his dick in and out of the eager throat, impaling Montana's head on his long, man-sized tool.

The tied-up cowboy slave looked down over his shoulder at the scene as Tom and Mat began to use this new hunky stud. He appreciated Montana's looks: a strong jaw, a firm aquiline nose, a heavy black moustache, bright green eyes, and a lithe well-defined muscular body covered with soft brown hair.

Mat pulled Montana's pants down around his ankles and wrapped his belt around them a couple of times. Now Montana knelt with a big cock fucking his face, his arms and legs bound tightly.

"Okay," Tom said, pulling his dick out of Montana's face. "We're gonna get that ass nice and red hot for me to fuck. I like to fuck an ass that's been well-prepared, and by well-prepared I mean hot, red, and bruised from beating."

Montana looked scared, but deep down he knew he could take it; he had before, in Berlin, when that huge uncut German

Master had bound him in a dungeon and whipped his ass with a leather strap. So he knew that if these guys wanted to beat his ass for their fun, that he could take it.

Tom and Mat dragged Montana to an old sawhorse in front of the hanging slave. The kid watched as they picked Montana up and hauled him face down over the sawhorse. They positioned him so that his ass was perfectly aimed into the air, completely vulnerable and ready for abuse.

Tom reached down and pulled the heavy leather belt out of the pants he had stripped off earlier. He wrapped one end around his hand and let the belt hang free in front of Montana's down-turned face. He teased the tip of the belt around his face, gently pulling the leather belt up along Montana's cheeks, then his neck, across his lips.

"See how nice and gentle that can be?" Tom said. "See what pleasure this soft leather gives you?"

"Yes, Sir," Montana said.

"You'll see what it feels like to get pleasure from this strap when it's beating your ass, too, dog." With that he stepped behind Montana, raised the belt and brought it down with a hard crack across his ass. Immediately a bright red welt rose across the untanned asscheeks. Montana felt his dick ooze pre-cum as the belt was brought down hard across his ass once more.

Tom kept beating the ass, each stroke of the belt delivering more pain, more red welts, more excitement to the helpless slave draped over the sawhorse.

"Like it?" Tom asked.

"Yes, Sir," Montana answered. "Beat my ass, man. Fucking beat it raw."

Tom needed no other encouragement. He lit into the ass with full force, slamming the leather belt across the ass, across the back of the thighs, the side of the hips, coming dangerously close to whacking the tip of the belt across the low-hanging balls.

Montana moaned in pleasure at being so brutally beaten. He wiggled his ass, trying to get more of the belt, more of the wonderful sting of the whipping. But as suddenly as he had started, Tom stopped, discarding the whip on the other side of the room.

Tom and Mat picked Montana up and turned him over, laying him on his back lengthwise on the sawhorse. His arms were uncomfortable underneath him, forcing his chest to curve up, as if his tits were being offered up for use. Mat untied his legs, pulled his pants off completely, and then secured each ankle to the two posts at the end of the sawhorse with leather straps. Now Montana lay stretched out flat on his back, his legs tied down, his full hard-on throbbing up against his belly, his big balls hanging between his legs, resting on the rough wood of the sawhorse.

Mat opened a can of beer, stepped up to the bound man and poured cold beer all over his body. He started by pouring beer on Montana's face, letting him drink some of it, then pouring a steady stream across his chest, belly, and then soaking the big cock and balls with the ice-cold beer.

"I can tell you like that yellow liquid on your body," Tom said, positioning his crotch over Montana's upturned face. "How about some hot yellow piss to warm you up from all that cold beer?"

Montana didn't have time to say anything before Tom let go a steady stream of hot piss, aiming it right into Montana's face. "Open up and drink it, asshole," Tom ordered, aiming the piss at Montana's mouth. Montana opened his mouth and drank Tom's hot piss, swallowing the salty liquid, feeling it burn in his throat.

"Yeah, man, that looks damn good," Mat said, coming up beside Montana and aiming his fat prick at Montana's cock and balls. Suddenly Montana felt a second stream of piss spraying over his legs and belly. He kept on drinking the steady flow of piss while Mat drained his bladder on his body, in short spurts, or so it seemed. He opened his eyes and saw that the suspended cowboy-slave was also pissing onto Montana's helpless body.

Montana went crazy at being pissed on by three hunky dudes. He sucked every drop of piss from Tom's dick, begged for more, and was disappointed when he didn't get it.

Tom and Mat had other ideas, though. Montana had barely

finished milking Tom's dick of the tasty piss before he was picked up and carried to the crate behind the slave. They put him on his knees on the crate, putting his face just inches from the hot fucked ass, dripping warm ass juice and cum.

Mat untied Montana's feet, spreading his legs as wide as he could without forcing Montana off the crate. He put his hand on the back of Montana's head and pushed his face into the crack between the slave's ass-cheeks. He took the belt and wrapped it around the boy's hips and the back of Montana's head, forcing Montana's face deep into the cleft between the cowboy's ass-cheeks. Montana couldn't pull his head away. He could smell the sweet smell of cum up the ass, a salty, sweet taste was on his lips.

"Eat that ass, man," Mat ordered. "Stick your fucking tongue up that fucked slave-hole and suck out my cum. I want you to drink my cum out of this kid's ass. Clean it up real good, drink all that cum, suck out that ass juice."

Montana did as he was told, sticking his tongue into the hot hole and then sucking on it, drawing the warm cum out of the slimy shit-chute. He slurped on the hot stuff, getting hornier by the minute as the ass yielded up what seemed like a cup full of cum and juice.

The next thing he knew was that Tom was rubbing some grease onto his tight asshole, lubing it up for the invasion of Tom's long love pole. Tom showed no mercy; he slapped the ass a couple times real hard and then forced his dick into the little hole and shoved.

Montana cried out in pain, but the ass in his mouth muffled all sound. Tom hauled off and slapped his ass again, and thrust his dick all the way up Montana's hole once more.

He fucked and fucked, grabbing Montana's hips and pulling him onto his dick. The asshole opened up and accepted the greasy cock, throbbing in and out of the hole.

"Yeah, baby, get that dick up there; take that fucking cowboy dick up the ass. I'm fucking a cowboy!"

Tom shoved his dick in as hard as he could, reveling in the feel of having a hot tight greasy ass wrapped around his long heavy tool. He bucked and groaned and slapped Montana's ass harder.

"I'm gonna prepare the slave," Mat said. Montana wondered what this meant, but he was busy eating ass and taking big dick up his butt. Montana was being impaled by this cowboy sword, being fucked like a goddamn dog.

Then Montana felt the belt loosen, his head set free, and then he saw that the slave-cowboy had been set free. He was stepping down in front of Montana, looking into Montana's wet piss and cum covered face. Suddenly, the slave spit in Montana's face. Montana did nothing; he was still being gloriously prodded up the ass.

He was amazed at the size and beauty of the slave. When he had been suspended by the ropes, it was hard to tell his dimensions, but now that he stood in front of Montana's face, he could see that the dude was a big strapping muscleman, with a cock and set of balls to match.

The slave leaned close to Montana's face. "I'm gonna fuck you with this big dick, too, man. You're so fucking worthless that even this cowboy slave can use you the way I want to!"

He shoved his big dick into Montana's mouth. His hands were still tied behind his back, so all he could do was surrender to the two raping cocks, invading him at both ends.

He sucked on the slave dick until it was fat and throbbing. Tom was fucking harder how, close to shooting his load. Montana sucked and thrust his ass back against the hard prick, squeezing his ass tight. He could feel Tom's buildup to orgasm, and in one heavy thrust, he felt his ass being flooded with hot cum. It almost felt like it was burning his asshole. It just came and came, pouring into him like a garden hose, until, spent at last, Tom withdrew his cock and offered the ass to the slave.

The boy walked around behind Montana and simply stuck his dick in the dripping hole. Montana gasped at the size of the throbbing organ; it was so thick that he thought it would rip him open.

"Whoa, man," Montana said, without thinking.

The slave shoved his dick really hard, and Mat came round in front of Montana and said, "What was that you said, boy?"

"Nothing, Sir," Montana said, sorry that he had momentarily resisted the heavy fucking.

"Nothing my ass," Mat said. "Looks like we're just going to have to keep your mouth busy enough that you don't have no time to say nothing at all."

Montana opened his mouth to take the big cowboy's dick, but Mat said:

"Shit, man, I don't want to get sucked. I just got done fucking that slave-boy that's fucking your ass. I gotta take another leak." Mat aimed his dick into Montana's mouth and started to piss. Montana swallowed the stinking liquid while he felt the hard fast thrusts of the kid cowboy's monster prick.

"Yeah, man, drink that piss," Mat said, "take that slave dick. Service us cowboy studs, man, service our thick dicks. You piece of shit, drink it all, and get ready to take the slave's cum."

Mat finished pissing into Montana's mouth and ordered the slave to quit fucking his ass. "Get that big dick out of that slimy hole and fuck his face. I want to see him drink your cum."

"Yes, Sir," the slave boy answered, moving to the front and dangling his fat prick in Montana's face. It was all shiny and dripping with grease, juice, and some bit of shit around the base.

"Suck it," the slave ordered, and then he shoved his dick into Montana's throat, grabbing the back of his head with both hands, locking them together and pulling his head onto his cock.

"Yeah, baby, it won't be long now. You're gonna feel that hot cum explode in your mouth." He fucked the face harder. "This dick was just up your ass, man, and now it's in your mouth. You like that? Think it's raunchy enough for an asshole like you?"

Montana perceptibly nodded his assent. Tom and Mat stood by watching, goading the slave to fuck Montana's face harder. They pulled on their softening dicks, now satisfied and hanging curved like horses. "Fuck his face," they said, "Shoot your load, boy."

The slave forced his dick all the way down Montana's throat and held it there, gently fucking the hot opening on the verge of orgasm.

"Oh, eat it, baby, suck that dick, oh man I'm gonna cum, I'm cumming, man, I'm shooting my load, oh, yeah . . ." The slave shot his hot sperm into Montana's throat. Montana gagged on the thick juice, but managed to swallow it all down, milking the fat organ with his lips to get the last drops.

"That was good!" the slave said, stepping back and shaking his dick. "What a mouth!"

Tom and Mat came forward and untied Montana's arms. They looked down at his rigid sex pole, pointing up at his belly, swollen and purple, demanding release.

"Okay," Mat said, "You've earned it. Go ahead and jerk off in front of us. We'll watch you do it, because we don't want to see any cum spilled on the floor."

"That's right," Tom said, "When you cum, just shoot it into your hand and then drink it down. You're gonna eat your own cum or you're not gonna cum at all? Got it?"

Montana was grateful for the chance to finally let his load go. He grabbed his big purple dick right away and started pulling on it, passing his hand over it faster and faster. He stopped for a second to spit in his hand, making it really slick to slide over his throbbing cock.

Mat and Tom and the slave-boy stood by watching Montana stroke his cock. He jerked off faster and faster, bucking his hips forward and arching his back, getting ready to shoot a big wad. Just as he approached the brink, he brought his left hand forward to catch the hot spunk.

With a long, low moan, he shot his load, squirting hot white cum into the cupped hand. He pumped his dick faster as the cum spurted in great globs into his palm. And then, aware that he was being intensely scrutinized, he brought his hand to his mouth, tilted his head back, and drank his cum. He licked his hand clean, and when he was done Mat and Tom came over and patted him on the back.

"That was alright, stud," they said, laughing and horsing

around. 'You live around here?" they asked.

"Sure do," Montana said. "I live just outside of Cheyenne on a big spread."

"Oh, yeah?" they said. "Sounds good. Need some company tomorrow night?"

"I just might," Montana grinned, "I just might at that."

PAINPLEASURE

I T IS WITH A SUDDEN intake of breath and a sharp stabbing
pulse that I always turn that corner into Ringold Alley in
San Francisco. I know what I want. One short alley, a hundred
men in leather, the dark obliteration of all reality in the dim
shadows of midnight mansex.

Sex with strangers in the middle of the night, any night—it
is aural, apocalyptic, abandoned. There is very little light. The
air is translucent, blurred, almost opaque. Until a match is
struck to a cigarette or leather snaps against flesh—a passing
moment of sensation prior to the certainty of . . .

The boots, the broken glass, the odor of garbage twist around
the cerebral registration, and then suddenly I breathe deeply of
the nitrite, proferred by a gloved hand. I smell the incense, the
black leather, and an indefinable aroma of masculinity. It closes
in on me, lifting me in a sudden rush, a physiological exhuma-
tion of my lust, peeling my attitudes into raw, naked need.

Fuck me. Sir. Please fuck me. The wave hits my head, my
chest, my groin, and the words rush out to span the chasm
between the leatherclad muscular form beside me and my pure,
honest cravings.

Fuck me. Now, here Sir. My head drops at just the moment
my wrists are seized and handcuffed. You asked for it, baby,
slave, you gonna get it. And I'm forced to my knees, my head is
yanked forward towards the two white globes framed in black

leather, and my tongue slides into the hairy velvet hole.

Eat it, slave-hole, worthless pig, piss-drinking slave. You get beat? You get worked over? Get your tits tortured? Get fucked hard? You drink piss?

Yes! But my mouth is clamped between the rock-hard cheeks, my lips fastened round the wet hole, my tongue poking the steaming shit-chute.

Oh, baby, you're gonna fucking get it real good all the fucking way while these other guys watch and cruise and spit on your slave body, waiting their turn. Eat it! Stick that tongue up there. Show me how much you worship my asshole. Show me how much you want to serve.

Turning, spinning, rocking backward, and a long cock pushes past my lips, passes over my tongue, slides down my throat, my nose buried in sweaty pubes. Pumping, ramming, choking, relaxing, and then the big tool pries my throat open, swallowing the cock-head, my throat an open tube for the big, fucking dick.

Impaled on a raping prick my head bobs up and down. Leatherclad fingers trace circles across my shoulders, my biceps, my pectorals, circling my erect tits and then suddenly, violently clamping them, twisting, pulling, tugging. My tits shoot pain-pleasure through my body, and the leather fingers pull harder, lifting my chest by the pink flesh. Still, the long wet manmeat forces its way in and out of my throat, ramming, stretching the tube wider and deeper.

The sound of flesh slapping flesh, a sudden sting and warm glow . . . My pants have been torn off and I am being beaten by someone behind me, out of my visual field. Again my ass is spanked, left, right, left again, dead center on the hole, then hard, violent right, left, hard, loud. My body twists erotically at the simultaneous beating and impalement, my own thick rod thrust proudly throbbing into the caressing cool night.

You fucking handcuffed slave. Suck that big dick.

But the pumping stops, the beating stops. All is without motion or sensation. A great silence emanates, rippling out in ever-larger circles of stillness, soaking calm into the concrete, macadam, brick. Slowly the silence is broken by the sound of a trickle, the golden sacrifice on the red altar of my tongue.

The piss streams thicker, stronger, flooding my mouth with salty warmth, tracing damp rivulets through my beard. I swallow and gulp, drinking deep of the spraying fountain, the curved dick hanging loose in my mouth, delivering a river of private caring, accepting my surrender of servitude, my desire to prove myself to the man above me: I can take it. The hot liquid floods my mouth and fills my stomach and I sense there is more than proof in the bargain: I want it, I need it, it is an ultimate edge.

The moment passes, and I am seized under the arms, dragged a yard to the gutter, laid out face down. A boot shoves against my ass, pushing my naked groin into the gutter. My rigid cock lunges against the concrete gutter, feeling the cool muddy dampness there. The boot works my legs farther apart and runs up and down the crack of my ass, between my legs, over my big ball sac hanging low in the gutter.

The boot draws away briefly, then hurls forward against my big nuts. Painpleasure drives through my loins, covering my body with sweat. I muffle my cry, gasping silently at the leatherman's abuse. I will not object; I have consented and given myself. I have asked for it.

Drops fall across my back, and I analyze the sensation to discover its source. Is it raindrops? Piss? Spit? It is, I think, more piss, a final christening of my upturned ass, a baptism of my vulnerability.

The handcuffs are removed, my hands are released. I am dragged forward in the gutter, my dick scraping against the concrete. My arms are pulled above my head, one cuff is secured to my right wrist. Then the short chain of the handcuff is passed over and behind the bumper of a black pickup truck, and my left hand is secured in the steel cuff.

Pulled upward, my body arches serpent-like from the rear bumper. The weight of my body presses heavily against my huge erect prick. I am captive. I am helpless. I am in slight and wondrous pain.

The leatherman straddles my ass, sitting down on my thighs and running his gloved fingers along my crack, finding the hot hole and pressing against it. The leather finger is forced into my mouth, my spit coating the long finger in preparation.

With no regard my ass is suddenly penetrated. The long fat leathered finger forces its way past the tight sphincter, demanding instant acceptance. There is no preparation, no warning before the finger is joined by the probing heat of pulsating manmeat, certainly and relentlessly prying my ass wide open.

Intensity of crossed sensations blurs my conscious speculation. A wave of lust and sensuality overtakes my mind, and I become prisoner of physical sensation, my cerebration completely numbed by the thrusts claiming my entire being.

The pounding at my ass continues; my ass is filled again and again with slamming meat, sending wave after wave of pleasure through my body. But a sound cuts through, slices a direct connection to activity very close. Metal scapes against concrete and then metal slaps against my chest. A trashcan is being rolled beneath my body, under my belly and hips, raising the impaled ass right up, sticking out into the cool night air. My cock pressed downward in a painful curve against the steel barrel. The two men have rolled it back further, pulling my arms tight away from the truck.

My own image comes to me as the long tool moves harshly against my upturned ass. My torso is stretched out flat and taut, my ass is rolled over the trashcan and being rammed by a huge hard-on. Men are standing in front of my face, now at crotch level. They are lining up, they are pulling their dicks, finishing cans of beer, and suddenly there is a stream of hot piss pouring into my mouth, and then a second stream of yellow liquid joins it, my mouth eagerly swallowing two beautiful rivers of urine. My ass is loose and wet, hot, soft, a velvet tube for fucking.

The slamming does not stop. I am a sensation of sliding, of pushing and thrusting, of slick openness to a union with something loud, hard, big, and violent. I am a sensation of emptiness being filled, of a hollow plaything filled with pulsing cock and shiny piss. A third man steps up, straddles my outstretched arms and lets loose with a stream of gold, matting my hair and beard with wet heat.

The emptiness flows in again; my fucker has gone. The trashcan is rolled away. A cold breeze passes over my bare asshole. Hands at my ankles grasp firmly. The roar of an engine draws near. Another truck stops behind me. The leatherman is at my wrists, unlocking the handcuffs. Two more men seize each arm. Rope is wrapped at my wrists, separately. Suddenly I am inhaling sex incense again, my body rushing upward, higher and higher, floating in a mad surge of lust.

I am suspended spread-eagle between the two trucks. My arms are far apart, my legs as far apart, tied to the front bumper of the second truck. The nitrite blurs my knowledge of what is happening. I feel hands, leather, spit, warm piss—all passing over my outstretched body, suspended above the alley.

Someone is pushing his cock into my ass again. My head has fallen back and a long prick is guided into my mouth, sliding effortlessly into the straight open tube of my throat. I am rammed from both ends, hands prying at my dick, tugging at my balls, pinching my tits.

I hear a vague command, some plan set into motion, and then I feel the result. My suspended body begins to arch upward at the insistent pulling of my tits and balls. I do not think, I do not calculate. I have delivered myself for use; I am a mouth and an ass; I am a set of mantools to be played with, to be abused, hurt, pleased. It pleases someone to whip my cock with a belt. It pleases another to fuck my face, shooting cum deep into my throat. Another is absorbed in squeezing my balls. Several flood my ass with hot cum, until it runs freely from my hole, providing slick lube for the next invading weapon.

Time is confused and absent. The use continues without stop. Perhaps I am used by only four men; perhaps it is fourteen. Or more. I cannot tell, I cannot count. My eyes see only balls slapping against them as hard cocks fuck my throat or pour streams of piss into my gulping stomach.

Suddenly the activity tapers, and a gloved hand is wrapped around my dripping throbbing prick. The fingers milk the tool, but my focus shifts to the fingers probing my loose hole, sliding in, pushing a hand inside my rectum. Short, brief—a moment of odd discomfort and pleasure ends with my ass clamped around a fat wrist.

The piss has stopped, the men have gone. There is but one connection here. It lifts me higher, beyond the dark clouds hugging the city, beyond the floating between two trucks, above the deep ache in my tits, in my balls.

He slides deeper and harder, more demanding, exacting my service, my cooperation, my complete and willful surrender to the bondage into which I have delivered myself. Images cross my mind—which registered only images and an unbearable sensation of fullness—and I rise higher by the moment. The clouds churn and boil, as if about to burst into flame. I see a pillar of fire, I feel the trucks move, though their engines are silent.

It builds, increases, adds one sensation to another, one image to the next, images of pricks, of red lights, or bronze bodies on a beach. I see a deep black void, I hear a muffled silence, and slowly a tingling numbness climbs into my body by way of my fingers, my toes, my face. The numbness closes in on my center, on the connected masculinity, and then there is no turning back, no reversal of the fate of my body, and the tingling is complete, translating itself into a violent thrusting of my hips down onto the invading arm, translating itself into a reverse bucking of my prick against the sky, and it flows in an explosion, I see an explosion, a scene of violent destruction, and I shoot myself into the sky, hurling fountains of white liquid at the gods, claiming my own divinity over the moment, my own transcendence of eternity, and as I shoot the final drops heavenward, he draws rapidly out of my ass, yanking free and clear. My prick yields its final lightning bolt at Zeus.